Content

Publication History

Samurai in the Kindle ebook of the same name.
Rickman's Plasma , Creature Feature, Ghostwriter Publications, 2009
Home is the Sailor , Holiday of the Dead, Wild Wolf Publishing, 2011
Turn Again , Null Immortalis, Nemonymous 2010
Inquisitor, Historical Lovecraft, Innsmouth Free Press, 2011
The Scotsman's Fiddle, Mountain Magic, Woodland Press, 2010
The Toughest Mile, The Game, Seven Realms Press, 2011
The Havenhome, High Seas Cthulhu, Elder Signs Press, 2007
The Yule Log, This is horror ezine, Winter 2011
Living the Dream, Watch, Phoenix Imprint Press, 2011
The Shoogling Jenny, Specters in Coal Dust, Woodland Press, 2010
The Haunting of Esther Cox in the Kindle ebook of the same name.
Dancers in The Weekly News newspaper in June 2007.
The Brotherhood of the Thorns in the Kindle ebook of the same name.
The Young Lochinvar in The Mothman Files, Woodland Press, 2011
A Slim Chance in A Cat of Nine Tales, Rookhaven, 2012

SAMURAI AND OTHER STORIES

By William Meikle

Published by Crystal Lake Publishing
www.CrystallakePub.com

Edited by Joe Mynhardt

Cover Design:
Ben Baldwin – http://www.benbaldwin.co.uk/

eBook Formatting: Robert Swartwood –
robert@robertswartwood.com

Samurai

Dawn broke as Duncan MacKenzie stood watching the remains of the *Dubh Glais* break up on the reef offshore.

They'd only just got into the longboat in time. In truth Duncan had little recollection of what had just happened. He'd been woken from a drunken sleep to the sound of splintering wood and raging wind. Big Bill had half-dragged half-carried him up onto deck, and the next thing he knew they were in the longboat and sculling for shore in the teeth of a gale with all the strength they could muster. The surf threw them onto a long shingle beach. They lost Dave the Bosun's Mate to the waves before they managed to drag the boat far enough up the shore to be safe. They turned just in time to see the *Glais* dashed into pieces on the rocks.

Only five men made it ashore.

Five out of fifty-five. 'Tis a pity the Captain had to be one of them.

Duncan had made the Japan run three times now, but this last journey had been made almost unbearable by the pompous little man who called himself the Captain. In reality Moorhouse was little more than a lawyer with good connections, and Sailing Master Douglas had done all the actual sea-faring that was required, while Moorhouse strutted and preened like a well-fed peacock. Douglas had gone down with his ship, but Moorhouse had ensured that he was first to the longboat, and first ashore. Now he started to bark orders. So far none of the other four had bothered to comply, and Moorhouse's face turned beetroot-red with anger and frustration.

"You need to get back out there, and salvage what you can. There are tens of thousands of pounds worth of silks and porcelain on that boat. And they are mine."

Duncan laughed.

"You go and get them then," he said. "I have no desire to get myself killed for some fancy plates and a frock."

"I demand that you launch this longboat," Moorhouse shouted. "I am your Captain." He drew his sword and waved it in Duncan's direction. "You have a clear duty, to my ship, and to me. You signed up for this."

"I signed up for service on the *Dubh Glais*. That duty is now done. And if you dare point that thing at me again I will shove it up your arse," Duncan said.

Moorhouse went even redder.

"I will see you flogged for that remark."

Big Bill walked up to the blustering little man. He was nearly a foot higher and twice as broad. He reached out and took the sword even as it was drawn back for a strike. Moorhouse immediately made a grab for it. Big Bill smacked him on the side of the head with the flat of the blade and the little man went down in a heap.

Big Bill tossed the sword to Duncan.

"Here you go, Duncan. A keep-sake for you. Now come on, lads. Let us see if we can find some shelter."

Duncan joined the other three as they walked off the shore leaving Moorehouse senseless on the gravel.

~-o0O0o-~

I am a man of honor. My duty, as it has always been, is as clear before me as the day I was called to it.

Before enlightenment, I chopped wood and carried water.

After enlightenment, I chopped wood and carried water.

I will serve, and I will protect.

There is nothing more.

~-o0O0o-~

John McLeod took the lead as they entered the forest that stretched right up close to the shore. Duncan was last to enter the woods. He walked behind Geordie McCann and used the man's bulk to try to get some shelter... to no avail. Even here under the trees the wind howled and whistled. Water dripped in near continuous streams from dank grey lichens that hung in tangles from every branch. Underfoot the going was sodden, their boots sucking moistly on the mud with every step. Duncan tried swatting some of the lichen aside with the sword, but that just set it swinging and dripping even more water. In the end he put the sword through his belt, lowered his head, concentrated on watching Geordie's back and took it one step at a time.

He almost walked into the man when they came to an abrupt halt.

"What is it?" he asked.

"See for yourself," Geordie said and stepped aside.

They had arrived at a ravine where an inland river reached the shore. A wooden structure sat high above them up a steep stone staircase carved directly into the cliff face. Even from his position far below Duncan could see that the woodwork was highly lacquered and covered in intricate carvings.

"A temple?"

"Aye," Big Bill said. "One of them heathen temples. But it is shelter, and that is what we need. Come lads. Let us see what kind of hospitality awaits us."

Big Bill took the lead up the staircase. The steps were treacherous – steep, green with slime and slippery underfoot. They were forced to go on all fours for long stretches, and Geordie McCann had his eyes screwed tight shut most of the way to avoid looking at the vertiginous drop. All four of them were exhausted and filthy by the time they dragged themselves over a last lip and lay panting on the ground.

Duncan's heart fell when he got his breath back and looked up at the temple. The wood was festooned with more of the grey lichen, and now that they were close, they could see places where the weather had won over the lacquer and eaten holes into the frame of the building. The whole place had a general air of aged decrepitude.

We will find no hospitality here.

"Chins up, lads," Big Bill said, getting the men to their feet. "At least it is shelter. And who knows what awaits us inside? We may yet be surprised."

And surprised they were. Although the outside of the temple seemed worn and decrepit, several of the inner chambers were still watertight. They walked through three echoing rooms, thankful of the shelter, and were beginning to think that the whole place was empty when John McLeod let out a shout.

"There's something here."

They had arrived at the dead centre of the building. In the middle of a polished lacquer floor sat a cauldron placed over a circular hearth of stone. Beside it was all they would need to make themselves welcome. There were three large stone jars respectively containing dried rice, beans, and water. At the foot of one of the jars there was a small wooden box containing tea-leaves, so strong that their scent filled the room as soon as the lid was opened. On the far side of the hearth they found cups, bowls and spoons, enough fuel to last for several days and a tinderbox to get everything going.

"Them heathen gods sure know how to treat their worshippers," McLeod said as he got a fire going in the hearth. Big Bill muttered to himself but said nothing.

Duncan was just glad to get some heat into his bones. It took a good twenty minutes, but soon the fire had warmed the room and the aroma of rice and beans cooking on the cauldron had them salivating. It was only after he felt warm and dry that Duncan looked around. Besides the doorway they had entered there was only one other exit from the room, a large ornate door on the other side of the chamber.

~-o0O0o-~

Once again intruders have come.

They will be fed and watered, as the old ways command.

Time will tell if they are true or false. But whatever the outcome, I will serve, and I will protect.

If you understand, things are just as they are.

*If you do not understand, things are just as they are.
There is nothing more.*

~-oOOOo-~

Moorhouse turned up just as the food was ready to be served. Green slime coated him from head to toe. He had lost his powdered wig at some point on the ascent, and his bald head shone with a mixture of rain and perspiration. His face was redder than ever and he almost fell in the door, his legs seemingly incapable to taking him a step further.

No one moved to his aid.

"I will have you *all* flogged," he said as he approached the fire.

Duncan laughed.

"Be careful, wee man," he said. "We have no meat, and yon cauldron is just about the right size for you."

Moorhouse looked around for help but he was ignored, the others being too intent on getting some hot food inside them. The little man took a bowl of rice and beans and took himself off to one side away from the others, eating in silence.

If truth be told, Duncan *did* feel a twinge of guilt. After so long on the ship taking and obeying orders it felt like mutiny to be so cavalier with the *Captain*.

But we are shipwrecked. The old order will not hold here.

Once the men had their fill of rice and beans they stewed some tea. The chamber had got warm and the air lay thick with smoke, but none of the men moved, all content to stay close to the fire. Above the crack of burning wood they could hear the drumming of rain on the roof, and none of them was keen to face the elements just yet.

Eventually talk turned to their predicament.

"We are not far off the shipping lanes," Big Bill said. "Once this rain dies down we can make a pyre. We are high enough here that it should be spotted soon enough. And we have food and water a' plenty to keep us until then."

The others agreed. All apart from Moorhouse. He'd been muttering into his food since he arrived, and now that he was dry and warm some of his old bluster had returned.

"As soon as the weather abates you will row out to the *Dubh Glais* and see what can be salvaged of the cargo."

Once more Duncan laughed.

"No. We will not. Mayhap *if* a rescue is forthcoming... mayhap then will we salvage *your* cargo for you, but until then, we stay here in safety."

Moorhouse looked ready to debate the matter, but a single glance from Big Bill put a stop to that.

The day dragged on. McLeod and Big Bill got into an argument about the best way to make tea, Geordie McCann cried like a baby, and Moorhouse sat in a corner muttering to himself about *rack and ruin.*

At some point Duncan curled up near the hearth and fell into a deep sleep

~-o0O0o-~

Now we draw near to it. I will bide my time, and let

them decide.

Sitting quietly, doing nothing, spring comes, and the grass grows by itself.

I will serve, and I will protect.

There is nothing more.

~-o0O0o-~

Duncan woke with a start. It was full dark outside, and only the fire illuminated the chamber. Geordie McCann was snuggled up close to him and snoring fit to raise the roof. Big Bill and McLeod were on the other side of the fire.

There was no sign of Moorhouse.

Now what is he doing?

Duncan grabbed for the sword and was reassured to find it still by his side. He rose, slowly, being careful not to wake the others. It was only when he stood that he saw the open doorway on the far side of the chamber. Moorhouse had gone to check out the other rooms.

Looking for a way to make a profit no doubt.

A dim light flickered in the room on the other side of the door. Duncan took the sword from his belt and crept forwards.

Two tall pillars on either side framed the doorway. The smiling faces of wooden foxes watched him as he passed through, their features flickering slyly in the firelight, their eyes dark and hooded. Duncan looked back at the hearth. The fire suddenly seemed even more inviting.

A creak, as of a door opening, came from the room

beyond, and his curiosity got the better of him. He stepped into the room.

The light was coming from a makeshift firebrand that had been placed in a sconce on the wall. The chamber was obviously the temple's main altar. High arches of black lacquered wood overhung a large plinth that was painted in deep reds and golds that seemed to shine in the light from the brand. Three large wooden chests sat on the plinth, and the sound Duncan had heard was Moorhouse opening the nearest one.

"So it is desecrating holy ground now is it?" Duncan said in a mock whisper.

Moorhouse turned, unable to hide the sudden guilty look on his face.

"These are heathens," the little man said. "It is no desecration if they do not follow the will of our Lord."

Duncan raised the sword.

"Nevertheless, you *will* stand aside."

Moorhouse eyed the sword warily, then pointed at the chest.

"There is gold here," he said. "More than enough for us all. More than enough to cover our losses on this trip."

Duncan laughed.

"Your losses you mean. Stand aside," he said and showed the man the sword once more. "I will not let you defile a temple."

A voice spoke behind him.

"Then you will have to stop us all," Big Bill said quietly. "For if there *is* gold here, then we will have it."

Big Bill, McLeod and Geordie all stood in the doorway.

Duncan focused on Big Bill.

If I can persuade him, the others will follow.

"You would not go into an Abbey and steal the monk's gold, would you Bill?"

Big Bill spat on the varnished floor.

"This is no Abbey. And we are beggars in this land, Duncan. In case you have not been paying attention, yon shipwreck made paupers of us all."

Duncan smiled sadly.

"I have rarely been anything but a pauper. If you are bent on this course, I will stand aside. I will not fight you, Bill, for you are my friend. But I will not help you in your desecration."

Duncan put away the sword and left the room to sit by the fire in the centre.

No good can come of this. Of that I am certain.

He heard Geordie's cries of delight as the boxes were opened. The sound of the chests being dragged to the ground and their contents scattered echoed through the temple.

~-o0O0o-~

It is decided then. I am called to act.
  I will serve, and I will protect.
  There is nothing more.

~-o0O0o-~

Duncan made more tea while the others counted up their *prize*.

Big Bill came over to where he sat.

"You can still have your share, Duncan," he said. "We shall all be rich men after this night."

Duncan shook his head.

"I prefer to stay a pauper."

Big Bill laughed. He held up a gold coin.

"The Captain says these are nigh on six hundred years old," he said. "And each one would buy a house in Edinburgh."

He dropped the coin into the top pocket of Duncan's tunic.

"I would buy you a house, Duncan," he said. "And mayhap, on our return, I will buy you a whole street of them."

The big man went back to fawning over the booty. Their laughter sounded too harsh to Duncan's ears. Dawn was starting to come up so he took his tea to the main door of the temple and looked out over the view.

From this height he could see the whole strait through which they'd been sailing when the storm struck. The wind had dropped and the rain eased to a steady drizzle. But the length of the strait was under a thick haze of fog. Even if they lit a fire, no one would see it.

He was about to report this to the others when he heard a dragging noise behind him. He turned to see Geordie and McLeod manhandling a chest across the floor. The polished boards showed white long gouges all the way through to the central chamber.

"Where the deuce are you going with that?" Duncan asked.

"To the longboat. The Cap'n says we need to be ready for rescue."

11

So he is the captain again is he? That did not take long.

Duncan laughed.

"Do you not remember the cliff steps? You will never get yon box down there. Not in one piece anyway."

The two men ignored him and made for the door.

They had just crossed the threshold when a dark figure stepped in front of them. It happened so fast that Duncan barely knew what he had seen. Something silver and bright *swished* in the air. The chest fell to the floor in the doorway. McLeod's left arm was still attached to the handle.

McLeod looked at the spouting stump at his shoulder. He just had time to register surprise when there was another *swish,* like a lightning bolt from a clear sky.

McLeod's head parted from his body and bounced away out of sight. The body slumped to its knees pumping blood over the treasure chest.

Geordie screamed and fainted dead away.

Duncan raised his sword but the black figure stepped to one side and was gone, as swift as a bird taking flight.

Big Bill ran up to Duncan's shoulder.

"What the hell did you do?" he said. Duncan stepped back and showed the big man his sword.

"It was not me Bill. Look. My weapon is clean," he whispered. "There is someone else here."

Big Bill went to move towards the door, but Duncan pulled him back.

"Wait. 'Tis not safe."

The big man looked at the body slumped in the doorway, then back at Duncan. He must have seen something in Duncan's eyes, for he nodded, and stepped back.

Moorhouse arrived at a run.

"What is going on here?" he shouted.

Duncan laughed.

"It seems someone does not want you leaving with the gold," he said.

Moorhouse looked down at McLeod's body and went white.

"You killed him?" Big Bill replied.

"No," he said. "Duncan is right. There is someone else on this island with us."

Moorhouse still looked suspicious. He stepped forward towards the chest.

The black figure reappeared in the doorway, standing, his legs apart, as if protecting the box. The man who stood there was even taller and broader than Big Bill, made even more imposing by his garb. He was clad head to toe in black polished metal and leather armour. The tall helmet rose into a peak above the lintel of the door, only dark slits showing for eye-holes. No part of the body was unprotected, from the banded combination of metal and leather around the torso reinforced by thick shoulder guards, to a long enameled apron hanging below his knees. Heavy shoes protected the feet and shin guards were tied from knee to ankle. Each piece of the main body armour consisted of a set of small iron plates lacquered to protect the material against rust and laced together by gleaming white cord.

A scabbard was slung over the shoulders and he held

the weapon, a long straight sword, across his chest.

The figure didn't speak. It didn't have to. The intent was plain.

None of us are leaving here any time soon.

~-oOOOo-~

I can wait.
That is what I do.
The world is ruled by letting things take their course.
I will serve, and I will protect.
There is nothing more.

~-oOOOo-~

Even then Moorhouse still looked like he might step forward.

"What is it that you want," the little man blustered. "If it is the gold, I will see that you get McLeod's share."

Duncan pulled Moorhouse away.

"He cares not for your gold," Duncan said. "And neither do I. I will not stay here and be party to any more death."

But when Duncan strode towards the door the black figure once again raised the sword.

Even I cannot pass.

Big Bill laughed bitterly.

"It seems we are *all* to share. Come. Let us at least get McLeod out of here."

The black figure allowed Duncan and Bill to drag what was left of McLeod away. They left the arm where it was, the white hand still grabbing the handle of the chest, for neither of them wanted to touch it.

After they had stored the body in one of the empty rooms they went back for Geordie who was still lying insensate by the door.

"Let us get him to the fire," Big Bill said. "At least we can keep him warm."

Moorhouse was still staring at the black figure guarding the door. "You cannot keep us here," he said. "We are on the King's business."

Duncan laughed.

"The King's business is worth about as much as a shite in this place," he said. He helped Big Bill drag Geordie away.

'Where are you going?" Moorhouse called after them.

"Back to where it is warm," Big Bill replied.

"But we need to get out of here," Moorhouse wailed.

"After you," Duncan said.

They left the little man at the entrance and half-carried, half-dragged Geordie to the hearth. Duncan stoked the fire and Big Bill got a pot of tea brewing.

"The Cap'n is right about one thing," the big man said. "We *do* need to get out of here."

Duncan nodded.

"It might well come down to a fecht with the man outside. I am not sure we can take him."

Big Bill stared into the fire before nodding. "I have seen his like afore. They are *Samurai* – fearsome warriors, bound by duty. Our only chance will be to catch him off guard."

I am not sure a man such as that is ever off guard.

15

They sat in silence, drinking tea and watching the flames.

Moorhouse joined them as they were on the second cup.

"He is still there," he said. "He will not respond to entreaties. 'Tis like talking to an excise man."

Geordie woke soon after, and almost immediately started to wail like a babe. Big Bill managed to soothe him, but Duncan knew it was only a matter of time before the crying would start again.

We need a plan.

Duncan left the others and did a tour of the temple. Moorhouse had been right. The black figure still stood in the doorway, so still that he might be a statue. Duncan ignored him and surveyed the other rooms. The sight of poor McLeod's ravaged body gave him pause, and he stood there for long minutes, saying a prayer for the man's soul before moving on.

He found what he was looking for at the rear of the temple, on the far side from the entrance door. The wood back here was more rotted than at the front, and weak sunlight showed through holes where the rain had got in.

We can kick our way out of here with little trouble.

He went back to tell the others of the plan that was brewing in his mind.

Big Bill had got a fresh pot of rice and beans going in the cauldron, and the aroma filled the temple. Duncan laid out his plan while they waited.

Two of them would kick out the back wall, make an escape and search for help while the others kept the black man busy. Duncan already knew that, as the best swordsman, he would be one of the two to stay behind. The argument came when deciding who should stay with him.

Duncan wanted Big Bill beside him, but Moorhouse would have none of it.

"I need the big man with me," he said.

The thought has never crossed his mind that he might be the one to stay.

Geordie surprised Duncan.

"I will fight by your side," he said. "Although the very thought of it has me pishing my breeks. McLeod was my friend. I will see him avenged."

Big Bill nodded.

"We have a plan then."

~-o0O0o-~

An end is near.

When the student is ready, the master appears.

~-o0O0o-~

Duncan started counting in his head as he left the hearth.

When he got to a hundred he stepped into the entrance doorway and stood over the chest, trying to ignore the drying blood that had splashed and splattered around it.

The armoured figure raised its sword.

"Let us have at it then," Duncan said and stepped forward. At almost the same instant he heard the loud splintering of wood from the other side of the temple.

The black figure sent his blade out in a quicksilver flicker that Duncan only just managed to parry as it was over his heart.

He stepped forward into a lunge that caught the other off guard, but the *Samurai* managed to weave to one side and the stroke cut a slice across the armour at his ribs instead of taking him through the heart. The *Samurai* stepped into the attack with renewed vigor so that Duncan was hard pressed to defend himself. The sound of clashing steel echoed around the room as each of them searched for an opening. Duncan was painfully aware that he was weakening faster than his opponent, and decided to try a risky feint, one that he had sometimes had success with on the training ground.

He stepped backwards, as if retreating before the attack, and let his right leg give under him, feigning a stumble and letting his sword hand go down towards the floor, looking as if he was going to use it to steady himself. As he hoped, the *Samurai* went for his suddenly exposed left-hand side. He ignored the descending blade, and, with a straight arm, punched his sword upwards, catching his opponent under the ribs and pushing through with a strike that pushed clean through the armour and cleaved the *Samurai's* heart.

"Die, you bastard," Duncan shouted.

The *Samurai* had other ideas. It stepped backwards fast and Duncan's sword slid from its body.

There was no sign of any blood.

Duncan was struck momentarily immobile by the incongruity, and that gave the *Samurai* a chance. Fast as a snake-strike the shining blade came up and headed straight for Duncan. He saw it coming, and knew he had no time to defend himself against it, no time even to move.

Geordie chose that moment to enter the fight. He threw himself forward between Duncan and the descending blade. It caught him on the left shoulder and cleaved a path through to his right hip with no more effort than if it had been cutting paper. Duncan tasted blood that was not his own in his mouth and almost gagged. The two pieces of Geordie's body fell apart with a moist sucking noise that Duncan knew he would hear for the rest of his life.

Which may not be too far away.

He got his sword up again just in time as the *Samurai* stepped into a new attack, faster this time, their blades flashing and clashing. Duncan knew he was at a severe disadvantage, both in the strength and weight of his sword and in the lack of armour.

And I took the booger through the heart. Yet still he fights.

In self-defence Duncan stepped back behind the treasure chest.

The *Samurai* went still, blade held across his chest.

In that moment of silence Duncan realized that he could no longer hear the noise of wood splintering from the rear of the temple.

Duncan blinked.

The *Samurai* no longer stood in the doorway.

~-o0O0o-~

Learning is a phenomenon of gold and dung.
  Before you understand it, it is like gold.

After you understand it, it is like dung.
I will teach them this very truth.
They will learn.

~-o0O0o-~

Duncan stood looking down at what was left of Geordie before a yell came from the far side of the temple.

Big Bill is in trouble.

Duncan stepped across the treasure chest and out into the weak sunlight, expecting at any moment to be attacked. But no such attack came.

He ran around the side of the building. Big Bill was struggling with the Samurai. He had stepped inside a swing of the sword and now grappled hand to hand with the armoured figure. The *Samurai* still held its sword, but Big Bill was a seasoned fighter, and had positioned his wrestling grip such that the sword was useless in this struggle. Getting to that position had, however, cost him dear. The big man had already taken a sore wound to his side. Blood ran in runnels down his tunic and breeches, and Big Bill's face was ashen, as pale as mist.

Underneath and behind the struggling figures Moorhouse was trying to drag one of the treasure chests through the hole they had made in the temple wall.

"Help me," the little man shouted.

Duncan had other priorities at that moment.

He stepped forward and raised his sword. He cut down, hard, a blow that would have taken a man's arm off at the shoulder. He cut through leather and steel and felt the jolt run through him, momentarily deadening his sword arm.

The *Samurai* did not flinch. It did not even register his presence. With seemingly no effort it lifted Big Bill off his feet. It dropped an arm, seemingly leaving a weak point which Bill immediately went for. But it had been a ruse. The *Samurai's* hand went straight to Bill's throat. It gripped, hard, and Bill's face went from white to red. He started to choke. His legs kicked, thrashing against the thick leather apron. The *Samurai* did not relent. The grip tightened.

Duncan lunged forward with the sword again, thrusting the point deep into the *Samurai*'s back.

Still it didn't flinch.

It *twisted* its grip on Bill's throat.

The big man's neck broke with a crack that echoed around the ravine.

The *Samurai* dropped Big Bill's body unceremoniously at its feet and immediately moved towards Moorhouse. The little man cowered beneath the dark bulky figure, hands raised in front of his face.

"I will give you half," he said, wailing. "Please. Take half."

Duncan had half a mind to let the attacker do his job. But the *Captain* had been right all along. Duncan had a duty, a sworn duty.

What kind of man would I be if I let him die like a trapped animal?

Even as the flashing blade came down, Duncan had stepped forward. His sword blocked the attack and Moorhouse scurried away.

Duncan heard the scrape as the *Captain* dragged the chest out of the temple, but by then it was too late to do anything other than fight for his life.

~-o0O0o-~

The Dharma is without life, because it is free of the dust of life.

It is selfless, because it is free of the dust of desire.

It is lifeless, because it is free from birth and death.

It is without personality, because it has no origin and no destiny.

There is only now.

I will serve, and I will protect.

There is nothing more.

~-o0O0o-~

The *Samurai* pressed an attack that took all Duncan's skill to repel, the silver blade flashing and spinning in a dizzying set of thrusts and slices. Duncan had no thought of attacking – everything was defence and parry, trying to keep the blade from vital organs. He took a deep slash to his left forearm and felt blood flow in his sleeve, but there was no time to assess the extent of the wound as the *Samurai* came on mercilessly.

From the corner of his eye Duncan saw Moorhouse drag the chest away. He retreated along the same path, keeping himself between the attack and the little man.

"For pity's sake man," Duncan shouted. "Leave the chest. Head for the longboat. There is no sense in dying for a bit of gold."

If Moorhouse heard, he paid no attention. He had already dragged the chest as far as the steps down the cliff and was trying to manoeuvre the box over the lip.

Duncan blocked a blow that was heading for his

skull and succeeded in gaining a second's respite.

"It is sheer folly," he shouted. "You'll never get that box down that flight alone."

Moorhouse laughed bitterly.

"Yet I must try, for there will be no life for me without it."

With that he pulled the chest over the lip and was gone from sight.

The *Samurai* pushed forward in another attack, and once more Duncan was forced to retreat. Soon he found himself backing towards the lip at the top of the staircase. He took one step down, then another. The Samurai was now high above him, raining blows down towards his head that Duncan was hard pressed to defend.

He descended as fast as he was able but quickly came up against Moorhouse and the chest.

"Let it go man," Duncan shouted. "Or we will both be dead in seconds."

Moorhouse didn't reply, merely started to drag the chest faster. Duncan could not turn to watch. The *Samurai* came after him, the sword coming down like lightning bolts. Duncan's whole arm was numb and his sword had been badly notched in many places, but he had no choice but to keep up the defence for as long as he was able.

The descent seemed to go on forever. Duncan took another long cut, just above the bicep in his right arm, and immediately he felt the strength start to drain from him.

"Faster!" he shouted to Moorhouse, then had to duck as the *Samurai* aimed a kick at his head. He stumbled, almost fell, and put his foot down to balance himself. Instead of finding a step, he found Moorhouse's hand, stepping down hard on it. Bones broke under his foot. The little man screamed then fell away, the scream ending in a distant thud.

Duncan risked a look.

The broken body of the *Captain* lay some twenty feet below. The chest lay on top of him. It had landed square on his head, crushing the skull.

Duncan looked up, expecting the attack to cease and the *Samurai* to go still once more, but the blows still came relentlessly, even when they reached the foot of the stairs.

His retreat became frantic, barely stopping the *Samurai* blade an inch from his heart.

I do not have much time left.

Once again Duncan allowed his right knee to crumple and he let himself fall sideways. The *Samurai* went for his unprotected side and Duncan took his chance. He thrust upward, a perfect stroke that should have disembowelled his attacker.

When he withdrew his sword it was shining and clean. The *Samurai* had not even slowed.

I cannot fight such a thing as this.

The next time the *Samurai* raised the sword Duncan did not defend. He let his own weapon fall to the ground and waited for death to come. The blow came down on his right shoulder and he heard the sword grate as it passed through his ribs.

Duncan felt strangely still and content as he crumpled to the ground.

The last thing he saw before blackness took him

down and away was the *Samurai* reach down and remove the forgotten gold piece from his tunic pocket.

~-o0O0o-~

I should be dead.

Duncan came back to a semblance of thought some time later. His view was limited to two thin slits in the darkness. He tried to move but he seemed to be restricted. He felt heavy and encumbered.

It was only when he saw the three chests stacked on the red and gold plinth that he realized where he was.

And what he was.

I will serve, and I will protect.
There is nothing more.

Rickman's Plasma

He would call it 'Soundscapes of the City,' and it would make him his fortune, of that Rickman was certain.

How could it fail?

All it had taken was a reconfigured dream machine. Courtesy of Dreamsoft Productions, a particularly skilled burglar, and the latest software from MYTH OS, Rickman's visions of bringing his music to the world were now that much closer to reality.

For the past forty nights he'd sampled and tweaked, taking the raw sounds that streamed into his loft apartment from the city outside. He merged them with his dream compositions and formed them into a holographic construct of sound and light and ionised gas, an ever-moving plasma bubble that hung like a giant amoeba in the centre of his room.

As they swam, his creations sang, orchestrated overtures to the dark beauty of the night.

It had been a long hard journey to this point. During those first few days everything was sharp and jagged, harsh mechanical discordances that, while they had a certain musical quality, were not what he needed... not if he was going to take the world by storm. The plasma had roiled and torn, refusing to take a permanent shape and Rickman despaired of what the city was telling him. Everything was ugly, mean-spirited. The music of the city spoke only of despair and apathy and his dreams didn't make a dent when he overlaid them.

Then he had his epiphany.

Aptly, it came to him in a dream.

It starts with thin whistling, like a simple peasant's flute played at a far distance. At first all is black. The flute stops, and the first star flares in the darkness. And with it comes the first chord, a deep A-minor that sets the darkness spinning. The blackness resolves itself into spinning masses of gas that coalesce and thicken great clouds of matter reaching critical mass and exploding into a symphony. Stars wheel overhead in a great dance, the music of the spheres cavorting in his head.

Rickman jumped from his bed and pointed his antenna upwards to the sky.

Almost immediately he got results.

The plasma formed a sphere, a ball of silver held in the holographic array. At first it just hung there in space, giving out a deep bass hum that rattled his teeth and set all the glassware in the apartment ringing.

Things changed quickly when he overlaid his dreams.

Shapes formed in the plasma, concretions that slid and slithered, rainbow light shimmering over their surface like oil on water. They sang as they swam, and Rickman soon found that by moving the antennae he was able to get the plasma to merge or to multiply, each collision or split giving off a new chord, the plasma taking on solid form.

But it still wasn't right.

The really good stuff only really started to happen this very night. He played back his previous recordings while keeping the antenna pointed skywards.

The plasma roiled.

The sounds became louder, more insistent, especially when he pointed at a certain patch of sky.

Soon he had a repeating beat going, with a modulated chorus above it that rose in intensity, and rose again as the plasma started to pulse.

He set his recorders going and started experimenting, feeding the recordings back to the plasma through his one thousand watt speakers, merging the sounds with the compositions from his dreams.

Within the hour the globe of plasma was responding to his dream overlays. When he played the recordings back at full volume the plasma swelled. The music grew, the chords overlaying each other in an orchestrated dance.

Rickman was so excited that he didn't notice that the walls of his apartment beat in time to the music.

Nor did he spot that when he turned his back, the plasma ball grew, stretching like an inflating balloon. Cobalt blue colours flashed and it *surged*.

Rickman was its first victim.

~-o0O0o-~

The cops arrived ten minutes later in response to a neighbour's complaint about the noise.

When they burst in the door a plasma ball of rainbow colours rose to dance in the air in front of them, a swirling aura of gold and purple and black.

The sound started.

It was low at first, almost inaudible, but it rose to a crescendo until their ears were buffeted with raucous, mocking, piping; a cacophony of high fluting that crashed discordantly over them.

Then the smell hit them, the foetid, unmistakable

odour of death that caught at the back of the throat and threatened to send their guts into spasm.

The cops ran.

They didn't look back, and all the time the crazed fluting danced in the air around them. They called for help; but each shout only brought a fresh *surge* in the plasma. The air above the plasma crackled with electricity, blue static running over the formless mass.

It dragged itself across the floor leaving a grey glistening streak of slime behind it.

Within the protoplasm things moved, detached bones flowing, scraps of clothing fused with unidentifiable pieces of flesh. The surface boiled in numerous small lesions that bubbled and split like pieces of over-ripe fruit.

But worst of all was the source of the fluting. A huge, red, meaty maw pulsed wetly in time with the cacophony.

The younger of the cops made it to the elevator and slammed the button. He screamed, frustrated, as the doors were slow in starting to move. He let them open just enough to slip inside before he turned to look for his partner.

She was less than two yards from him, arms outstretched, pleading. He began to move towards her when she stopped and was jerked backwards like a marionette. Her mouth opened wide into a scream and she fell forward, her right hand hitting the *down* button even as he stretched out vainly.

The door began to close and, no matter how much he strained at it, he was unable to stop it from shutting completely and he could do nothing but watch the events in the hallway beyond through the small window.

The plasma had caught her by the ankle. Oily colours flowed across her body, the protoplasm gripping her tight.

She struggled hard to no avail.

Their eyes met, just once. Her mouth opened as if she was trying to speak, and that was when the swirling blob engulfed her head and the noises from her throat ceased to sound human.

The protoplasm *surged* again, and suddenly the window of the cab was coated with slime.

The cop gagged and fought hard to keep down the bile as a human foot, still trailing bloody threads behind it, floated across his view.

She was the second victim.

~-o0O0o-~

The cop spent the next fifteen minutes persuading his superiors that there was a problem in the tower block. In that time the plasma ate the little old lady in number 621 who played her radio too loud, the three kids jamming on electric guitars in 437 and the family in 223 who had been watching the latest Disney animation on their 60 inch TV screen.

By the time the cop's backup team arrived it had already filled the whole of the ground floor public area. The cop made sure he was first back through the door, but what met him made him step back immediately.

The floor was covered by a shimmering rainbow blob nearly four feet thick. There were things embedded in it – blood and hair and bones and eyes, all jumbled like a manic jigsaw, fused and running in to one another as if assembled by a demented sculptor. And in the middle of the floor something rose up out of the mass, a forearm stripped to the bone, skeletal fingers reaching for the roof. On each fingertip a grey, opaque eyeball stared blindly out at him.

That wasn't the worst thing though. The worst thing was the way the bones of the wrist cracked and groaned as the hand turned, the fingers flexing and bending as all five eyes rolled in bony sockets and stared straight at him. The mocking cacophony of high fluting crashed discordantly over him.

He raised his gun and fired.

The noise echoed loudly in the hallway.

The plasma surged again, enfolding the cop until he fell into it, like a drowning man going down for the last time. The plasma rolled forward forcing its way out onto the sidewalk beyond.

The backup team saw what happened to the cop. They started in with their own weapons.

The air filled with the noise of gunfire.

The plasma *surged* and took them.

Sirens blared as the squad cars of more backup teams arrived in the street.

The plasma *surged* and took them too.

~-o0O0o-~

The mayor got involved ten minutes later. Assembled in his room were the chief of police, the mayor's press officer and the chief of the fire service.

"So what is it doing now?" the mayor asked.

"Still growing," the chief of police answered. "And still feeding." The policeman was white as a sheet, and visibly trembling.

"How many casualties?" the mayor whispered.

"Too many to count," the press officer said. "It has covered three blocks... and we don't know if anybody is still alive in the area."

"That's it," the mayor said. "Call in the National Guard... and somebody close that window!"

Outside, the crazed fluting of Rickman's plasma filled the air.

~-o0O0o-~

People screamed.

The plasma *surged*.

It took thirty minutes to muster the National Guard. In that time, the plasma spread by five blocks in every direction.

If there was a noise, it consumed whatever made it. Trucks, people, dogs and subway cars, all fell under the surging protoplasm, and all served to feed its exponential growth.

The National Guard brought in jeeps.

The plasma ate them.

They brought in choppers.

The plasma ate them... protoplasmic tendrils shooting skyward to suck the machines out of the air.

The Guard used bazookas.

The plasma *surged*, and suddenly, the Guard were gone.

The city was full of noise.
The plasma fed.

~-o0O0o-~

The president got involved twenty minutes later. Assembled in his room were the chief of staff, the head of Homeland Security and the director of the FBI.

"So what is it doing now?" the president asked.

"Still growing," the head of Homeland Security answered. "And still feeding." He was white as a sheet, and visibly trembling.

"How many casualties?" the president whispered.

"Too many to count," the chief of staff said. "It has taken most of New York State... and we don't know if anybody is still alive in the area. It will be here in minutes."

"That's it," the president said. "Call in the Air Force. We're going to nuke it... and somebody shut that window!"

Outside, the crazed fluting of Rickman's plasma filled the air.

~-o0O0o-~

The plasma lay along the eastern seaboard covering most of New York and New Jersey.

Flocks of birds cawed and fluttered.

The plasma ate them.

Three passenger jets inward bound from Europe passed overhead at thirty thousand feet.

The plasma threw up tendrils and ate them.

The bomber carrying the nuke came in at over a thousand miles per hour.

The plasma ate it.

The nuke exploded creating a fireball of white heat and radiation at more than a million degrees centigrade.

The plasma ate it, *surged,* and headed for Canada.

~-o0O0o-~

The president of the European Union got involved an hour later. Assembled in his room were the heads of the UK, France and Germany. The president of Russia was on a TV screen, linked in by satellite.

"So what is it doing now?" the president of the EU asked.

"Still growing," the Russian president answered. "And still feeding." He was white as a sheet, and visibly trembling.

"How many casualties?" the president whispered.

"Too many to count," the prime minister of the UK said. "It has covered most of North America and is heading south and east fast... and we don't know if anybody is still alive anywhere. It will be here in minutes."

"We only have one option," the president said. `We hit it with every missile NATO and Russia have, and hope for the best. And somebody close that window!"

Outside, the crazed fluting of Rickman's plasma filled the air.

~-o0O0o-~

Over a thousand nuclear weapons were launched in the next fifteen minutes... enough firepower to start, or finish, a global war, enough mega-tonnage to destroy every city on the planet.

The plasma ate them all and *surged.*

~-o0O0o-~

The last human beings on the planet got involved an hour later. Assembled in a lab at the South Pole were scientists from the US, Brazil, France and Germany.

"So what is it doing now?" the Brazilian asked.

"Still growing," the head scientist answered. "And still feeding." He was white as a sheet, and visibly trembling.

"Is there anybody left?" someone whispered.

"I doubt it," the Frenchman said. "The last we heard it had covered the rest of the planet and was heading south fast."

"We only have one option," the head scientist said. `We keep quiet, and hope it passes."

The crazed fluting of Rickman's plasma filled the air.

The scientists sat in silence, barely breathing.

Their generator kicked in noisily.

The plasma *surged.*

Home is the Sailor

I smoked too many cigarettes, sipped too much Highland Park and let Bessie Smith tell me just how bad men were. For once thin afternoon sun shone on Glasgow; the last traces of winter just a distant memory. Old Joe started up "Just One Cornetto" in the shop downstairs. I didn't have a case, and I didn't care.

It was Easter weekend, and all was right with the world.

I should have known it was too good to last.

I heard him coming up the stairs. Sherlock Holmes could have told you his height, weight, shoe-size and nationality from the noise he made. All I knew was that he was either ill or very old; he'd taken the stairs like he was climbing a mountain with a Sherpa on his back.

He rapped on the outside door.

Shave and a haircut, two bits.

"Come in. Adams Massage Services is open for business."

At first I thought it was someone wandering in off the street. He was unkempt, unshaven, eyes red and bleary. He wore an old brown wool suit over a long, out of shape cardigan and his hair stood out from his scalp in strange clumps. I've rarely seen a man more in need of a drink.

Or a meal.

He was so thin as to be almost skeletal, the skin on his face stretched tight across his cheeks. I was worried that if I made him smile his face might split open like an over-ripe fruit.

"Are you Adams?" he said as he came in. He turned out to be younger than I'd first taken him for, somewhere in his fifties at a guess, but his mileage was much higher. "Jim at the Twa Dugs said you might be able to help me."

I waved him in.

"It's about time Jim started calling in some of the favours I owe him. Sit down, Mr...?"

"Duncan. Ian Duncan."

He sat, perched at the front of the chair, as if afraid to relax. His eyes flickered around the room, never staying long on anything, never looking straight at me.

"Smoke?" I asked, offering him the packet.

He shook his head.

"It might kill me," he said.

I lit up anyway... a smell wafted from the man, a thick oily tang so strong that even the pungent Camels didn't help much.

Time for business.

"So what can I do for you, Mr. Duncan?"

"I'm going to die sometime this weekend. I need you to stop them."

I stared back at him.

"Sounds like a job for the Polis to me," I said.

He laughed, making it sound like a sob. He took a bundle of fifty pound notes from his pocket and slapped them on the table. I tried not to salivate.

"No. This is no job for the terminally narrow-minded," he said. "I need somebody with a certain kind of experience. *Your* kind of experience."

Somebody put a cold brick in my stomach, and I had a sudden urge to stick my fingers in my ears. I got the whisky out of the drawer. I offered him one. He shook his head, but his eyes didn't stray from the bottle. I poured his measure into a glass alongside my own and sent them chasing after each other before speaking.

"And exactly what kind of experience do I need to help you?"

A good storyteller practices his tale. At first, when he tells the story, he sounds like your dad ruining his favourite dinner table joke for the hundredth time.

Oh wait... did I tell you the horse had a pig with him?

But gradually he begins to understand the rhythm of the story, and how it depends on knowing all the little details, even the ones that no one ever sees or hears. He knows what colour of trousers he was wearing the day the story took place, he knows that the police dog had a bad leg, he knows that the toilet block smelled of piss and shit. He has the sense of place so firmly in his mind that even he almost believes he's been there. Once he's done all that, he tells the killer story, complete with unexpected punch line.

Then there's the Ian Duncan method... scatter information about like confetti and hope that somebody can put enough of it together to figure out what had happened to whom.

I raised an eyebrow, and that was enough to at least get him started.

"It was four years ago we bought the hotel in Largs."

"Well there's your first mistake," I replied, but he didn't acknowledge me. Now that he'd started the story, he meant to finish it. The tale he told would have been outlandish to anyone else's ears, but like he'd said, I knew better, from bitter experience.

I let him finish – sick customers, ancient curse and all, before asking the important question.

"And how do you think I can help?"

Just telling me the story had taken it out of him. I forced a glass of whisky on him – it was either that or watch him die in the chair. He almost choked on it, but managed to keep it all down before replying.

"Come down for the weekend. There's a room I need you to see. Maybe you'll be able to make sense of it where I can't."

I *wanted* to say no, but he'd put his money on the table, and that got him my attention. Besides, his story had me intrigued, and I hadn't been *doon the watter* to Largs since I was a lad.

What better time than a holiday weekend?

~-o0O0o-~

Largs is where old people go to die – a Victorian seaside resort that is itself dying slowly of neglect. The Vikings tried to sack it eight hundred years ago. Maybe it would have been better all round if they'd succeeded.

I'd spent many long weekend trips here as a lad. My parents couldn't afford to go any further afield, and to a young boy one beach was as good as another, even if the weather was rarely good enough to take advantage on the long patch of golden sand to the south of the town. As I got off the train I could already see that the place hadn't changed much. It was raining, that steady drizzle peculiar to the west of Scotland, the kind that you just *know* is going to last all week.

Luckily I didn't have to go far. Duncan had given me instructions before leaving me in the office, but I could have found it with my eyes shut as it was on the sea front, two hotels down from the Barrfields theatre and next to the putting green where my dad used to swear for Scotland.

The Seaview Hotel lived on past glories from the days when the middle class of Glasgow filled it every weekend of the summer. Back in the twenties it had been the height of fashion, but now it exuded the faint whiff of decay. It was a rambling, Edwardian building, with thirty rooms and nearly as many corridors. The décor was all mock-Scottish; dark furniture, stuffed stag heads and heavy on the tartan for wallpaper and carpets; a hideous red and yellow that clashed with everything else in the hotel.

Duncan met me in the hallway and led me through to the dining room. There were six patrons sitting at a table by the bay window, and not one of them looked like they were going to last out the day, being as thin and wasted as Duncan.

"What's going on here?" I asked.

Duncan led me to the far side of the room.

"I told you," he said. "The curse..."

I waved him away and lit up a smoke. It improved the smell, but not by much. "Aye. The curse," I said. "Some time in the Twenties you said?"

He kept his voice low. "Jim McLeod was an old Navy man. He retired to Largs with his wife and had this place built. It was to be their dream home, but she died before it could be finished. After that McLeod became a collector," he said. "And he wasn't fussy about where he bought his pieces. Many of them were stolen on order from other collectors or museums. The story goes that someone took umbrage and laid a curse on the whole hotel."

I nodded.

"But here's what I don't get. Why now?"

Duncan didn't reply, but I saw a look in his eyes I recognised. He was hiding something. And he was afraid to the point of abject terror. I took pity on him.

"Let's cut to the chase. Show me this room you told me about, and we'll see if we can get to the bottom of this."

~-o0O0o-~

The room at the highest point of the hotel was packed wall to wall with antiques. Even to my unpractised eye I knew there was a small fortune just lying there in the accumulated dust. From the look of things McLeod's passion had been African tribal masks, and a variety of them leered down from the walls interspersed with weapons and beaded necklaces. But the thing that Duncan had brought me here to see was spread out under a pane of glass in a long display case.

At first glance it looked like a crude map, tracing a journey across Africa, ending at the mouth of the Zambezi river.

"McLeod thought it belonged to David Livingstone," Duncan said. "But I can't see it myself. Livingstone was a devout man of God. He wouldn't have anything to do with this depravity."

I saw what he meant as I leaned for a closer look.

What I had taken for paper was in fact skin, so thin as to be almost translucent. I didn't have to ask the question.

A map made on human skin, drawn in blood.

I had a good look at it, but it seemed I had already got as much information as I was going to get. Duncan was looking at me expectantly.

"Well, what do you think?" he asked.

I was still unsure exactly what he wanted from me. Sure, the curse *seemed* to be working... residents in the hotel were certainly wasting away beyond even what you'd expect in a pensioner's graveyard like Largs.

But how could I find out why?

I only knew one man who might help, and I was loath to involve him. I'd damaged my good friend Doug enough in too many cases. He was at his happiest right where he now spent most of his time, deep in the stacks of the Hunterian Museum storerooms.

I sent him a couple of pictures by email from my cell-phone, knowing even as I hit *Send* that it might be some time before he got back to his desk to receive them. In the meantime, I needed to maintain the illusion that I knew what I was doing.

"Let's have a chat with your guests," I said to Duncan.

He looked shocked at the suggestion.

"That might not be such a good idea," he said, but he allowed me to lead the way back downstairs.

~-o0O0o-~

My plan to interview the guests came to nothing, mainly because two of them were dead face down in their soup, and the other four were too far-gone to notice.

Duncan showed little concern, and only became agitated on my mention of calling the Police.

"There's no need for that, Mr. Adams," he said. Once he'd written me a cheque for an extra five grand I came to agree with him. I helped him drag the bodies out of the dining room. It took little effort – the old folks weighed no more than a small child at most.

Duncan had me take them out the back of the hotel and left me alone for a minute – long enough for me to wonder if the five grand was enough.

To either side the adjoining hotels had bowling-green flat lawns, lush and verdant. The Seaview on the other hand looked like someone had ploughed the lawn over, leaving lumps and bumps across the whole surface. It was only when Duncan came back with two shovels that I realized why.

Duncan held out a shovel but I ignored him.

"Just how long have you been burying guests out here?"

He wouldn't meet my gaze, and mumbled, but I caught the vital word.

Years.

"Please," he said, holding the shovel out to me, his eyes pleading. "No one need ever know."

But I will.

I left him to it and went in search of a drink.

~-o0O0o-~

One advantage to an almost empty hotel is that the bar

is quiet, and a man can smoke with impunity. I helped myself to a large Scotch and lit up a Camel. By the time I got on to the second Scotch I was starting to feel more myself, and the large cheque in my pocket had me feeling much more sanguine about the situation. I thought matters had improved when my phone beeped and I got a text message from Doug.

No real idea beyond burning it, it said.

Burning it. There's a thought.

I took a third Scotch upstairs with me. I checked out the window when I got to the top room. Duncan was still out on the lawn, knee-deep in a growing hole. I was about to burn his property, but then again, he'd brought me here to stop the curse, and that's what I intended to do.

I had to take a spear from the wall to prise the glass case open, having to slice and chip at glue that had gone rock hard. I'd finished the third whisky by the time I was done, but finally I was able to lift the lid.

The thing felt slimy to the touch, almost warm. It got warmer still as I flicked the Zippo and applied the flame to a corner. It took fast – so fast that it went up with a *whoosh* and I had to drop it to avoid getting singed. I stood back as it blazed itself down to a charred black mass on a now equally charred carpet.

I was feeling pleased with myself... right up until the screams rose up from out in the back garden. As I moved to the window my phone rang. I answered it on the way, just in time to read the full transcript of Doug's text that had been split into two messages.

"No real idea beyond burning it... would not be recommended."

Bugger.

Things got even worse when I looked down from the window.

Duncan had backed away, holding a shovel like an axe, smacking it again and again on the head of one of the recently deceased.

Or maybe not so deceased.

The withered thing pushed herself upright, shakily at first, then more sure of herself as she started to stagger forwards. There was more life in her now than there had been before she *died.*

Duncan hit her again, screaming in fury.

"Die you old bitch, die," he shouted. The old woman tripped, but didn't fall. She opened her mouth and clacked her teeth together. The effect was spoiled when the false top set slipped out and fell wetly to the grass, but she didn't slow. Duncan screamed one last time then fled for the back door of the hotel.

I should have gone to his aid, but I was dumbstruck by the view below me.

The whole lawn seethed and roiled, as if a great beast struggled to break through the blanket of grass. But this was no single beast. The first indication was a pale arm bursting with some force through the sod, grasping for a hold. More arms pushed through; some pale, some grey, some green and moist with decay, but all grasping.

I remembered Duncan's answer when asked how long he'd been burying bodies.

Years.

Even as they dragged their re-born bodies up out of the lawn, screams rose up through the hotel from below.

I grabbed the spear I'd used to open the display case and made for the stairs.

~-o0O0o-~

Duncan was once more the source of the screaming. I found him in the rear scullery, fighting to hold the back door closed against a press of bodies. They were packed tightly around the door, a crowd of what looked like over twenty, coming forward slowly. At first all that could be seen were silhouettes, dark shadows against the strong daylight beyond. But when they approached the glass door, it became all too clear what they were.

They had once been pensioners, but they'd been too long in Largs... far too long. Some of them were in better condition than others were, but all shared one common, open-mouthed expression, teeth and gums working in expectation of food.

The outside door of the bar crashed open and the press of bodies fought in a scrum trying to reach us.

"Bastards!" Duncan shouted, as the first of them pushed into the scullery itself.

It had once been a woman, dressed in an expensive tweed two piece suit and Gucci shoes. Now she missed one of her heels. She lurched from side to side like a drunken sailor.

I stepped forward and slammed the spear into her chest.

She staggered backwards, but only for a second. By the time she came forward again three more of her kind had pushed through into the scullery.

I felt something tug at my arm. It was Duncan.

"Mr. Adams," the hotel owner said. "I really think we should be going."

I shoved the old man ahead of me and headed for the door at the far end of the scullery. We barrelled through it at the same time. Duncan kept going down the corridor beyond, but I stopped, trying to lock the door behind us. The handle turned in position, all the way round three hundred and sixty degrees. There was no way to lock the door.

Well, this just keeps getting better and better.

I backed away down the corridor. The door swung open, slowly, revealing the scullery beyond. The undead already filled the room. Unblinking stares looked for fresh meat... and found me.

They shuffled forward. I stabbed with the spear, twice, thrusting deep into dry flesh. The attackers didn't flinch. I thrust again, deep into the belly of a fat thing that had once been a formidable woman. She *sucked* it in, and the spear was torn from my hands. I turned and ran, catching up with Duncan in the dining room. He was backing away from the table by the window where four more of the *things* shuffled from their seats. Alive or dead, I didn't know, but it made no difference – they all looked at me with that same *hunger* I was coming to recognise.

"Outside or the stairs?" I heard Duncan say. "They're at the front door already."

"Take the stairs," I said.

Once more we took the stairs almost together, all the way up to the collections room at the top of the building. I slammed the door behind me, but again there was no lock to secure it.

"Shit."

We're trapped.

Outside, footsteps thudded as the undead came up the stairs.

I threw my weight against the door.

"Find something to wedge it. Quick."

I locked out my legs and leaned into the door, trying to put my weight just over the handle. Something heavy hit the other side, hard enough for the door to open by two inches then slam shut again.

Behind me I heard clattering and smashing.

"If you're going to do something, now would be a good time," I shouted.

The door slammed against my shoulder, opening almost three inches this time.

"Let it open further next time," Duncan shouted.

"Open further? Are you mad?"

"Trust me. I have a plan."

The next time the door slammed against me I let it open slightly wider.

Duncan stepped forward and threw something through the gap, something that smashed in the hallway beyond.

I put my shoulder to the door and slammed it shut. This time Duncan helped me.

"Okay," the older man said. "Now I need your lighter."

I managed to dig inside my jacket, came up with the Zippo and handed it to Duncan.

"If I say duck, don't ask 'Where?'" Duncan said.

The door slammed hard on my shoulder. My feet slid on the floor as the door opened, six inches, then nine. A long dry hand at the end of an arm clad in thick blue serge gripped the inside edge and pulled. A head followed, grey hair hanging lankly over a face further obscured by a full salt-and-pepper beard. The blue serge was a heavy jacket, done up with silver buttons.

A naval man.

I heard the distinctive sound of a Zippo being fired up.

"Duck," Duncan shouted.

I ducked. Something flew past my ear, something that burned yellow.

The hall beyond the door exploded into flame. The blue-serge clad figure fell away from the door. I slammed it shut and Duncan wedged a chair under the handle. Even though the door was firmly closed the smell of cooking meat seeped through the gaps.

"Good plan," I said when I'd caught my breath. "What did you use?"

He looked sheepish.

"A bottle of Smirnoff. Blue Label. I hid it up here so the missus wouldn't catch me at it."

That was the first I'd heard of a Mrs. Duncan. I wasn't sure I wanted to ask, but I had to. "And where is she now?"

He waved at the door, fresh tears in his eyes. "Out there for all I know. I put her out in the garden nearly a year ago now. But if I know her she'll be up and about – she never missed a chance to give me a hard time."

My phone rang, saving me from having to get deeper into the conversation. It was Doug.

"How's it going?" he asked. In reply he got a thirty-second diatribe on the merits of not splitting up text messages. I may even have used several words my mammy wouldn't have liked very much. Even then, he wasn't particularly contrite, but I couldn't afford the satisfaction of hanging up on him – Doug was our only chance to get out of this.

"Come on then," I said when he showed no signs of replying. "I know you. You wouldn't have phoned if you didn't have something for me."

"McLeod was a naval officer," Doug began.

I didn't have time for the long version. Something had started pounding on the door again, rattling it in hinges that looked old and rusted.

"I know," I said. "I've met the man. Very sprightly, considering he's been dead these many years."

I heard Doug's sharp intake of breath.

"And have you seen the collection?" he finally said.

"Seen it? I'm standing in the middle of it."

I didn't have to see him to know he was smiling.

"That's good," he said. "You need to find her hair."

"Her?"

"Mrs. McLeod. He had her scalp and hair made into a headpiece after she died. There was a great scandal and..."

"Enough," I said, feeling as if I'd just kicked an excited puppy. "Just get to the point Doug. The undead are at the door, and they're worse than the bible-thumpers."

The pounding at the door got louder as if to emphasize my point. The top hinge squealed, the screws starting to loosen in the sockets.

I sensed his smile had faded, but he did speed up.

"It's a talisman," he said. "Part of a Zulu

necromancy ritual. It's used in conjunction with..."

"Let me guess... a map written on human skin?"

"Right first time. And now that you've burned one, you have to burn the other. If you don't all those affected by the curse will arise and walk the earth and..."

"Yadda yadda yadda. I've seen the movie," I replied. "Anything else I need to know? Like why this is happening now?"

"Well old McLeod has been in the ground a while now. Maybe this is a last attempt at bringing his wife back before he is too far gone?"

Just at that the door decided it had taken enough of a beating and gave way beneath the assault. The first thing to come through was an arm clad in blue serge – badly singed, still smoking, but unmistakably belonging to McLeod.

"I'll get back to you on that one," I said. I threw the phone aside and tried to put my shoulder against the door. "Find a wig," I shouted at Duncan. "It belongs to his wife."

Then I was too busy to talk for a while.

~-o0O0o-~

It felt like someone was hitting me on the back with a large lump of wood... in fact, someone was. McLeod's hand gripped at the edge of the door and *tugged*. I had to slam my weight back against the door, hard, to keep him out.

Too far gone my arse.

"What exactly am I looking for?" Duncan called.

"How the hell should I know? Just burn anything that looks like hair."

The weight behind me pressed even harder and I buckled. A withered hand grabbed at me, and I had to leave a clump of hair behind as I pulled away. The door fell in with a crash.

"I've found it," Duncan shouted at the same moment.

I had to back away as McLeod came through the doorway, those who had paid for his obsession shuffling close behind.

"You'd better be right, wee man," I said. "Quick. Where's the Zippo?"

That was when I remembered.

He threw it out into the corridor.

But hardened nicotine addicts aren't stupid enough to be out without a backup plan. I held McLeod off with one hand and fished a box of matches out of my inside pocked with the other.

McLeod's teeth *clacked* perilously close to my fingers.

I threw the matches in Duncan's direction, hoping he was quick enough to catch them.

Then I was in a fight for my life. McLeod showed no sign of being too far-gone for a fight. He took my best punch, right on the point of the jaw. His head rocked and a split appeared in the skin of his neck, gaping bloodless and grey. It didn't slow him any. He came inside my swinging arm and grabbed me. He forced my head to one side and exposed my neck. Then he sniffed, twice, close together, as if checking my after-shave.

"Where is it!" he said.

His voice was rough, harsh, almost a bark.

I tried to speak, but the grip around my throat was so tight that all I could manage was to keep breathing.

"Where is it!" he said again, almost shouting this time. His breath smelled, of stale food and stagnant water, but I guessed now wasn't a good time to tell him.

With his spare hand he went through my pockets; fast and methodical, like a pro. When he didn't find anything, the hold on my throat tightened further still. I tried to break the grip, but my strength was going fast. I punched him, hard, just below the heart; he didn't even wince.

He laughed in my face.

"Is that all you've got, lad?"

He threw me away, like a discarded rag. His hand barely moved, yet I flew, a tangle of arms and legs, crashing hard against the far wall and falling to a heap on the floor. Something gave way in my lower back; a tearing pain that I knew meant trouble.

I hoped I'd live long enough to see it.

I turned to see him coming for me again. I held up an arm, but in truth I had no fight left in me. McLeod came on, teeth *clacking*.

~-o0O0o-~

Duncan saved my life.

Just as McLeod reached for me, his minions right behind him, a forest of arms my only view, I heard Duncan shout.

"Is this what you're looking for?"

McLeod turned away from me, and I had a clear

view across the room as the case came to its denouement.

Duncan had what looked like a long wig in his left hand, and a burning candle in his right.

"Burn it," I shouted.

But it looked like I was in no immediate danger. The undead were all focussed on Duncan. Nobody moved, the only sound the sputter of the flickering candle.

"Burn it!" I shouted again.

Duncan had other ideas.

"I know how you feel," he said to McLeod. "Every day, I want her back. Every day I miss her. But look at yourself, man. Do you want her back like this? Could you stand it? Here..."

"No!" I shouted, but couldn't stop him handing the wig to McLeod.

"Let her go," Duncan said softly. "Set both of you free."

McLeod didn't move, just stood there stroking the hairpiece as Duncan put the candle under, first the wig, then the navy man's long beard.

He went up like a piece of dry paper, consumed to ash in less time than I would take to smoke a cigarette. At that point I expected the others with him to fall to the ground, or wither and turn to ash themselves.

That's how it works in the movies.

But this was Largs, on a holiday weekend. Things didn't work like in the movies around here. The undead milled around the room, seemingly devoid of purpose, maybe twenty of them in various states of decomposition.

"We should burn these too," I said, but I knew

already my heart wasn't in it, and I was glad when Duncan disagreed with me.

"Just leave them to me," he said. "I'll take care of them, like I've always done."

By the time I left he had them all in the dining room, sitting over cups of tea that would never get drunk, fancy teacakes that would never get eaten.

That's Largs for you.

Turn Again

She walked down to the Promenade most days to check on progress. The wind-farm was going up fast, despite all the protests and hot air in the local press. After an initial flurry of excitement at the start of construction the townspeople *harrumphed* and went back to their more mundane concerns, leaving Patty as one of the few still interested in the new forest rising offshore.

In recent days she had noticed the older man. He was always on the same bench and never spoke, just nodded as she passed.

It was on the day that the fifth propeller was lifted into place that he did more than nod. He touched the brim of a battered hat, lifted it several inches, and bid her a good morning. That was enough to get them started.

Over the coming weeks she found Mr. Tullis to be an excellent conversationalist and a keen student of local history. Indeed, he had an almost encyclopaedic knowledge of so many subjects that she thought him to be a retired academic.

They never spoke of their own situations, for which Patty was grateful, but they did become friends, of a sort, and Patty found herself hurrying to the promenade each morning for her newest flash of enlightenment.

On the fiftieth day their talk finally turned to Mr. Tullis' personal history. Patty knew that this was a turning point. Soon she would have to speak of herself, and at that point, their relationship would be changed forever. But for now, she was content to sit and listen to the old man.

He started in his usual round about way, by drawing attention to the wind farm.

"The last one goes up today," he said. "Bringing our little meetings to a conclusion. I have grown fond of you, lass. And I owe you an explanation."

She did not ask the obvious question, afraid to break his flow.

"I have been sitting here these past weeks, watching the farm grow, and considering the metaphors. As I have watched these shores all these years, so shall these wonders of science watch, drawing their circles in the sky in much the same way that I began, with my circles on paper."

He turned and took her right hand in his. After all these days of polite distance there was something faintly erotic in the act and Patty felt her cheeks flush.

"I am not what I seem," Mr. Tullis said. "Then again, what is?"

He smiled sadly, then took a small leather bound book from his pocket. He opened it and showed her an illuminated diagram done in red, black and gold in a precision worthy of Durer.

It was titled *MALAGMA*, and showed a fiery red serpent eating the world which was depicted as a shining golden disc.

"Strictly speaking," Mr. Tullis said, "this isn't part of the process at all, rather, this is a symbolic representation of the whole. *Malagma* is Latin, meaning *Amalgamation.* The whole process, the quest if you like, is to amalgamate the soul, the *microcosm*, with the universe, the *macrocosm*."

"Sorry," Patty said, trying a smile. "You've lost me already."

Mr. Tullis laughed. "I thought I might. Fourteenth century symbolism was obscure even then."

He thought about it for a short while. "Do you know anything about Zen?"

It was her turn to laugh.

"Only from re-runs of *Kung Fu.*"

"Well, grasshopper," Mr. Tullis said. "Everything is one, and one is everything."

"*I am he as you are he as you are me and we are all together?*" Patty said.

"Yes," he replied. "We are the egg men. All together in one huge womb that is the universe, the *macrocosm.* Alchemists were convinced that mercury transcended both states, both above and below, both life and death. It came to symbolize the transformation required to reach illumination and eternal life."

"Illumination?"

"Let's not get ahead of ourselves," Mr. Tullis said, smiling. "I just wanted you to get some idea what we're getting into."

He stared out at the windmills. "You know, I haven't been happy for a long time. When I began, I truly thought that this was what I wanted. But I have seen everything I love wither and die. No matter how many platitudes I use to console myself, no matter how *cosmic* the thought that my molecules might see the death of the sun, I am lonely. I have been lonely for *so* long. But seeing these circles being drawn in the sky gives me hope." He turned the page.

CALX was the heading. The pictures showed a young

man, bound to a burning wheel by hands and feet in a figure X. He was smiling.

"You see? More circles. *Calx* is latin for Lime," Mr. Tullis said. "In this case, it means, *calcination*, or the process of purifying by heating. If you burn a body hot enough, it goes black, then, if you burn it even hotter, the ash turns white. Similarly, if you heat limestone, you'll produce a white powder that the Romans called *Calx Vita* or quicklime. This was considered a magical material, for, if you poured water on it, it gave out heat. Effectively, giving the heat back to the giver."

"And now I'm lost again," Patty said.

"This one's easy," Mr. Tullis replied. "Look at the picture. Fire purifies. It's also a code that says, in effect, make quicklime. It will give heat back to the giver. And, beyond that, it symbolizes the fact that the adept must purify his soul before continuing. Wheels within wheels yet again."

He tapped at the picture.

"This is from Greek mythology. *Ixion* was punished by Zeus. He tried to seduce *Hera*, and for his presumption was bound to a perpetual wheel of fire. But Ixion had seen the face of the Goddess, and although in eternal pain, was also eternally happy. Everything can be seen from two angles. Everything has at least two meanings."

He closed the book. "I burned on a wheel... centuries ago now. You are the first in many years that has even paused to listen. And I know why. You know all about wheels and death... don't you Patty?"

"Oh, Jenny. I should never have let you play on that bike." She started to cry, softly at first, then great heaving sobs that racked her whole body. The man merely sat and watched with eyes full of compassion.

"I could tell that you will see her again, in a better place," he said when Patty calmed. "But I am by no means sure that is true. What I do know is that nothing is ever wasted. There *are* wheels within wheels. My own have finished turning in this meat suit I wear. I have been a ghost inside it for too long.

"I will leave you, as I myself was left, with two words, and this book. Turn again."

Patty looked down at the book as he put it on her hands. When she looked up again he was gone.

Far out on the water the last of the turbines started to turn.

Inquisitor

From the journal of Father Fernando. 16th August 1535

The time has come. It arrived yesterday from the New World in the hold of the *Santa Angelo* and it has been brought to the castle. The Inquisitor General has tasked me with discovering the true nature of the abomination, to make a full and careful examination and ascertain what manner of *Inquisition* might be made. It is a great honour, and one which I will fulfil with all the diligence the good Lord hands to me.

There is a certain doubt in my mind, a cloud that has hung over the proceedings since I read Juan Santoro's journal last night. A dark evil is detailed in those pages, and although the Inquisitor General teaches us that all things are powerless before the truth of our Lord, I have grave misgivings about the thing I am about to see for the first time.

I have prayed for strength, but still my knees feel like water and there is a cold pit in my belly that nothing can assuage.

However, my duty is clear.

It is time for the questioning to begin.

From the journal of Juan Santoro, Captain of the Santa Angelo, 3rd April 1535

If there is a hell on Earth then surely it is in this place here. No God fearing man should have to face the horrors I have led my crew through on this day. I give thanks that I have brought us all back safely to the ship, and I am much afeard with the thought of the return voyage, for the cargo is most foul and ungodly. But I would be remiss in my duty to the Church if I did not report on the things that plague this new land. If the Crown wishes, as I have been told, to colonize this place, then we must know what manner of things lay claim on it at present.

In truth, I know not what we have found. The natives died bravely defending it, and for most of the day we thought that we had stumbled on a great treasure. We fought through their defences, hacking and slashing our way through the savages to the centre of that dark temple.

As I have said, we expected treasure. What we found was beyond our ken. I have had it sealed in a lead casket, and will take it back to Seville.

But the journey will be long, for already it whispers in my mind, and I fear my dreams will be dark indeed during the long months at sea ahead.

From the journal of Father Fernando. 16th August 1535

"Already it whispers in my mind."

I had given no thought to that phrase, believing it to be the product of a sailor's superstition. But now, having seen my new opponent, I know better.

When we opened the casket that had been brought to the chamber where the questioning was to take place, I originally bethought that we had been played false and that trickery was at work. At first glance the lead box seemed empty, its bottom a dark shadow. But as Brother Ferrer leaned over it, something *surged* within, and he was forced to step back so suddenly that he knocked over a brazier and sent coals skittering on the flagstones. The blackness that rose from the casket, a thick liquid which had the consistency of pitch, seemed to rear back at that, giving me time to slam the lid closed on the obscenity.

And that is when it happened.

There was a *tugging* in my mind, a probing of an intelligence. I knew immediately what it was doing, as it is my own profession also. Even as I sought to ascertain the form of my opponent, at the same time it was questioning me.

I am not the only inquisitor here.

And there was something else, something I am loath to relate here lest it is discovered and my sanity is brought into question. I only caught but a fleeting glimpse, just as the lid of the lead casket dropped back into place, but it was unmistakable. As the black thing *oozed* to the bottom of the box a single eye, pale and smooth as a duck's egg, opened... and blinked.

From the journal of Juan Santoro, Captain of the Santa Angelo, 29th May 1535

Calamity has overtaken us, as I feared it might.

The thing has plagued our dreams since the start, and the crew has been without sleep for many days. There have been mutterings of mutiny since the beginning of the month, and last night matters came to a head. Three crewmen took it upon themselves to rid us of our tormentor.

At least, they tried.

Their screams in the dark alerted me to their plight and I was first to enter the hold. It is hard to describe the fear that gripped me as I saw the carnage the thing had wrought on my men. It was obvious that they had lifted the casket, probably intending to throw it overboard. But someone had dropped their end – that much is also obvious from the dent in the leftmost edge. I can only surmise that the jolt opened the casket – and let the beast out.

What did not need conjecture was the fate of the men after that.

The black ooze lay over the bodies like a wet blanket – one that seethed and roiled as if boiling all across the surface. Pustules burst with obscene wet *pops* and flesh melted from bone even as the men screamed and writhed in agony.

Their pain did not last long. All too soon the blackness seeped in and through them until even their very bones were liquefied and, with the most hideous moist *sucking,* drank up by the beast, which was now three times larger than previously. It opened itself out, like a black crow spreading its wings, the tips touching each side of the hold walls.

All along the inside surface of the *wings* wet mouths opened, and the air echoed with a plaintive high whistling in which words might be heard if you had the imagination to listen.

Tekeli-Li. Tekeli-Li.

My every instinct told me to turn and flee. But there

was nowhere to escape to except the sea itself, and that was a choice no sailor would make. Instead I stood my ground while Massa, stout coxswain that he is, brought forth some firebrands. Only then did the thing seem to cower and retreat, and only then did I remember the circles of burning oil which we had crossed on entering the black temple in the jungle.

I called for a barrel of pitch and tried to hold the beast at bay with a brand until aid might arrive. My adversary had ideas of its own. Now that it was free of the casket its powers had increased. It probed at my mind, searching for my weaknesses, taunting me with my dreams. I saw things no man should have to see as I was shown the atrocities that had been committed in this thing's name by the savages in the temple.

The grip on my mind grew stronger.

I saw vast plains of snow and ice where black things *slumped* amid tumbled ruins of long dead cities.

My head swam, and the walls of the hold melted and ran. The firebrand in my hand seemed to recede into a great distance until it was little more than a pinpoint of light in a blanket of darkness, and I was alone, in a vast cathedral of emptiness.

A tide took me, a swell that lifted and transported me, faster than thought, to the green twilight of ocean depths far distant.

I realized I was not alone. We floated, mere shadows now, scores – nay, tens of scores of us, in that cold silent sea. I was aware that other sailors were nearby, but I had no thought for aught but the rhythm, the dance. Far below us, cyclopean ruins shone dimly in a luminescent haze. Columns and rock faces tumbled in a non-Euclidean geometry that confused the eye and brooked no close inspection. And something deep in those ruins knew we were there.

We dreamed, of vast empty spaces, of giant clouds of gas that engulfed the stars, of blackness where there was nothing but endless dark, endless quiet. And while our slumbering god dreamed, we danced for him, there in the twilight, danced to the rhythm.

We were at peace.

A flaring pain jolted me back to sanity. I smelled burning skin, but took several seconds to note that it was my own hand that had seared. The coxswain, stout man that he is, had broken the hold on me by touching his firebrand to my skin.

I had no time to thank him, for the beast had encroached closer to me while I dreamed, and even now threatened to engulf me.

Once again I held the firebrand ahead of me, and with the aid of the coxswain I held the beast at bay, struggling to keep its grip from settling on my mind. Indeed, if the barrel of pitch had not been brought, I might have succumbed.

Burning the pitch enabled the recapture of the beast to proceed more rapidly. The heat from the flames threatened to set fire to the deck of the hold itself, but I refused to allow the men to put it out until we had driven the beast back into the casket.

I have ensured that the box is sealed completely, and it is now stored at the furthermost end of the hold. All I can do is keep the crew as far away from it as is possible on this small vessel.

That, and hope that in our dreams we do not fall

again under its spell.

But it is hard. For every time I close my eyes I dream, of vast empty spaces, of giant clouds of gas that engulf the stars, of blackness where there is nothing but endless dark, endless quiet. And while my slumbering god dreams, I dance for him, there in the twilight, dance to the rhythm.

In dreams I am at peace.

From the journal of Father Fernando. 17th August 1535

Captain Santoro's journal has at least given me a place to start. I already knew that s*trapado* would not be an option for this particular miscreant. Nor would I be able to utilise the rack or the maiden. But fire would be more than sufficient for my purposes. It took little work to prepare the cell for *Inquisition*, as matters are already set up amply for the ordeal. I ensured that the lead casket was placed inside concentric circles of oil such that they could be lit immediately in the event of an attempt to escape. I also had a brazier full of coals at hand to my right side and three needle-pokers burning white hot in a small oven to my left.

Even before I opened the casket I felt the *tickle* in my mind but I pushed it away. My God is stronger than any heathen devil. I mouthed the *Pater-Noster* as I lifted the lid.

Once again the black ooze surged, and the tickle in my mind turned to an insistent probing. Memories rose unbidden in my thoughts; of summer days in warm meadows, of lessons learned in cold monastery halls, of penance paid for sins.

I was under questioning.

That I could not allow. I am master of this inquisition. Several wet mouths opened in the black ooze. Using a pair of pliers I plucked a hot coal from the brazier and as another mouth formed I let the coal drop inside.

The grip in my mind released immediately, replaced by a formless scream which quickly became a chant that echoed around the cell. I knew the words. I had read them in the captain's journal.

Tekeli-Li. Tekeli-Li.

A long tendril reached from the lead box, coming towards me. I took a poker from the oven and with one smooth strike thrust it through the black material. The ooze retreated, shrinking back as far into the corner of the lead casket as it could get.

I leaned forward, a fresh poker in my hand.

"Are you guilty?" I asked, and stabbed down hard.

The *Inquisition* proper had begun.

From the journal of Juan Santoro, Captain of the Santa Angelo, 17th July 1535

Will this nightmare never end?

The beast, despite its incarceration, has steadily increased its hold on us since we forced it back into the casket. We cannot allow ourselves to sleep, for when we do we are trapped in its spell, lost in the dream somewhere above the cyclopean ruins.

In truth, the dream is seductive, even more so than drinking endless flagons of wine or constant inhalation of the weed that the natives smoke in the New World. Three of the crew have succumbed, falling into a deep slumber from which they cannot be awakened. They breathe, and their eyes are open, but I cannot get them to eat, and they are already close to starving. I fear they will be long lost afore we reach port.

Some days I almost feel like joining them. I am kept awake by a suffusion made from a roasted bean, a drink we discovered among the native tribes where we landed in the New World.

Would that were all we discovered.

Some of the crew have reported that the beast is also reaching into their minds during waking hours. Many of them have had the same compulsion – to go down into the hold and open the casket, releasing the thing to roam the decks. No one has yet given in to the demands, but it is another reason to make for port with all speed.

I know not how much longer we can hold.

From the journal of Father Fernando. 25th August 1535

It has taken more than a week, and sorely tested the Inquisitor General's patience, but finally, after I have burned away more than nine-tenths of its matter, it has weakened. I have found that the mind-grip works both ways. If I concentrate hard I can catch glimpses of what the beast is thinking, and feel its fear.

I have put it to the *inquisition*, and it has answered me.

As shocking as it seems, the beast has no conception

of our Lord. Indeed, it seems never to have encountered a single Christian, despite the fact that it is possibly the oldest living thing on the face of the earth. That revelation came as something of a shock to me. The creature has memories going back to a time when ice covered the face of the earth. Its first encounter with man shows a savage race clothed in furs with only rudimentary speech, and I am at a loss to know how such a thing can be reconciled from what I know from my study of the biblical texts. I must seek guidance from the Inquisitor General, for my thoughts are troubled and dark.

This beast I have under my ministrations is devious and subtle. It works constantly at me, testing my belief with scenes of lust and debauchery; maidens in states of undress displaying themselves wantonly for my pleasure, hot blood flowing to feed my growth. I have to see these things, and endure, for in the seeing I also learn more about the beast's drives and passions, which are mightily strong.

I had almost come to believe that this might be the most ancient of evils, the great deceiver himself. But the thing has memories even older than the time of ice, memories of a time when it was but a servant of something vast and strange... memories of a *creator* that I do not recognise as being anything resembling my Lord. I am at a loss to know what to think of this new information and must question the beast further.

I have learned one other thing. The *creators* gave it a name, a moniker by which it recognises itself. It is known as *Shoggoth*.

From the journal of Juan Santoro, Captain of the Santa Angelo, 14th August 1535

We will make port on the morrow. It matters little, for the dream is with us now in every waking hour, and no distance from the beast will make any difference. It has passed on to us so completely that we will never be free from it. Nor would we wish anything other. Indeed, I am not the only one who has found himself standing over the lead casket just to be closer to the blessed drifting peace it offers.

There is no pain in the dream, no fear, no hunger, just the sweet forever of the dead god beneath.

I have talked to the crew. We will do our duty and take our captive to the castle. But we will no longer work for the Church after this task is done. I intend to set sail again as soon as night falls. There is a spot in the South Seas where a dead god lies dreaming.

We will find him, and join him there.

From the journal of Father Fernando. 25th August 1535

I wish now that I had read Santoro's journal a mere hour sooner, for them I might have been able to prevent the *Santa Angelo* slipping out of port under cover of night, and I might have been able to question the crew as to the nature of the malady that so sore afflicted them.

For I too have been dreaming.

I am not alone. We float, mere shadows, scores... nay, tens of scores of us, in a cold silent sea. I am aware that others are near to me, but I have no thought for aught but the rhythm, the dance. Far below me, cyclopean ruins shine dimly in a luminescent haze. Columns and rock faces tumble in a non-Euclidean geometry that confuses the eye and brooks no close inspection.

And something deep in those ruins knows I am there.

But it is of no matter. The beast is now in my thrall, and its secrets shall be mine before the day is out. They will have to be, for I fear I have been lax in my *inquisitions.* Even as I have been burning my will into the beast's flesh, so it has been leaving its mark on me. This morning at my ablutions I discovered a fleck of blackness betwixt thumb and finger that no amount of scraping will shift. It has now covered most of my left hand, forcing me to wear a glove lest it is discovered. For if the Inquisitor General were to find out I am *tainted*, my questioning would be brought to an abrupt end, and that I cannot allow.

The beast *will* reveal its secrets.

I will begin again as soon as the irons are hot.

By order of the Inquisitor General, 28th August 1535

It is our command that on this day of our Lord the twenty and eighth of August that such parts of Father Juan Fernando that can be safely transported shall be taken to the place of the *auto-de-fe* and burned at the stake alongside the blasphemy which has afflicted him with its heresy.

It is further commanded that if the *Santa Angelo* is found in Spanish waters it should be set aflame and sunk with all hands and that no man is to touch any part of it under pain of himself being subjected to ordeal by fire.

Any persons found spreading the sedition of the *Dreaming God* shall be subjected to the full force of the *Inquisition*.

Let this be the end of the matter.

The Lord wills it.

The Scotsman's Fiddle

The Scotsman came over the pass in the Spring of '89, our first visitor after the hardest winter on record. Tommy Jeffries saw him first, when he had just crossed the Eastbrig over the Powell. By the time the wagon started on the last slope up to the eastern reaches I, along with most of the town, had come out to watch his progress up the valley, wondering about the occupants. Talk ranged from a new family out of Boston, to dynamite for the new mine-workings, to the Haberdasher that many of the women of town had long looked for.

When he pulled into what passed for our main street, he proved to be both more, and less than had been hoped for. A tall stocky man with a full black beard and hair flowing in a swathe over his shoulders stood up at the reins. He started his spiel as soon as he brought his wagon to a halt, his thick accent immediately apparent.

"Duncan Campbell is my name," he said. "And I am here to fix what ails you."

By now almost everyone from the town who wasn't down the mine had gathered to hear him. The scenes painted on his wagon told us more – the town had its first ever Travelling Show, all the way from Scotland. There were pictures of rivers and valleys; painted warriors running through heather and tall stone castles on rocky shores. He saw us looking.

"Behold," he said, his voice booming. "The same rocks you have here underfoot have travelled through the very earth all the way from the homeland. In aeons past we all came from the same place. Indeed, many of you here have even more recent good Scots blood in you. I can make that blood sing for you. I can bring you home."

He drew something from the folds of his coat. All of us present could instantly recognize it – a fiddle, nut brown and faded with great age. A second movement produced a long stringed bow.

The Scotsman took hold of the instrument and raised it to his neck. Before starting he looked out over us. The small crowd went quiet. When he spoke, it was barely more than a whisper, but it carried to each of us, as clearly as if he were a preacher on the pulpit.

"Breathes there the man with soul so dead, who never to himself hath said, this is my own, my native land?"

He started to play. I was expecting *Leather Britches* or *Wind and Rain*. What I got was something else entirely. I did not find out until later that each and every person present shared my experience.

His bow moved across the strings, setting up a drone – and beneath us the old rocks sang in recognition. As his tune began, the stones started to dance. I felt it first through the soles of my feet, but soon my whole frame shook, vibrating in time with his rhythm. My head swam, and it seemed as if the very walls of the town buildings melted and ran. The wagon receded into a great distance until it was little more than a pinpoint of light in a blanket of darkness, and I was alone, in a vast cathedral of emptiness where nothing existed save the dark and the dance from the fiddle.

Shapes moved in the dark, wispy shadows with no

substance, shadows that capered and whirled as the dance grew ever more frenetic. I smelled fresh flowers, and was buffeted, as if by a strong, surging wind, but as the beat grew ever stronger I cared little. I gave myself to it, lost in the dance, lost in the dark.

I know not how long I wandered, there in the space between. I forgot myself, forgot my friends, in a place where only the dance mattered.

I have never felt more complete.

When the dance stopped it was as if my heart had been torn from its root and I felt bereft, felt the loss as keenly as I had the death of my mother three years before. Tears coursed down my cheeks. As I wiped them away I heard sobbing from the women nearby.

I blinked and looked to the wagon – but it was no longer in front of us. A large tent that hadn't been there before was pitched beside the church. The Scotsman stood at the entrance in front of a chalkboard. It read: *For one night only. Entry 25c.* There was no explanation as to *what* we might be paying for, but I knew that we would all be there that evening.

And evening was closer than we thought. The morning shift was already making its way up out of the mine, faces and hands grey with grime, eyes deep set in their skulls with long ingrained tiredness. They found a crowd of townsfolk looking around in bewilderment.

We had been gone for nearly two hours.

That fact alone was enough to queer Malone the mine owner against the newcomer – six men were late for the afternoon shift and Malone docked them a whole day's pay. I do believe the Irishman might have tried to ban us all from attending that night's show for fear that it might disrupt the next morning's work. But, powerful as he was, and tight as his grip was on the town, the pull of that fiddle was stronger still. By the time we gathered in front of the tent at sundown we were all present – not just those who had heard the Scotsman play, but everyone else in the town as well. They had seen the effect on the rest of us, and even Malone was there, standing across the street and observing proceedings with a critical eye.

A box had been provided to collect our money at the entrance and we shuffled in. The tent somehow seemed much larger inside than its exterior suggested. Rows of pews, like church seats, sat in front of a small raised stage. I did have a fleeting thought that there was no possible way all of this had come up the hill in the wagon we had seen, but all other thoughts were secondary to the anticipation. I was going to hear the fiddle again, and I could hardly contain my excitement. I could see by the eyes of those around me that they were of the same mind.

An audible sigh of disappointment ran through the crowd as the Scotsman stepped up on stage without the fiddle in his hands. A hood obscured his features, and his face sat in deep shadow as he walked to the front of the stage and stood above us.

"I am the *Dubh Sithe*," he shouted. "And we are gathered tonight to open the way... with music."

From far off came the sound of a solo fiddle.

"... with magic... "

He spread his arms wide, clenched his fists, and when he opened them again two crimson birds, each the size of a large gull, rose from his palms and fluttered away towards the roof of the tent.

"But mostly... with blood."

He snapped the fingers of his right hand, and the red birds *burst* as if they had been shot. An arc of blood sprayed towards the front row of seats. Even as the audience cowered away, he waved his hand, and instead of being drenched, softly falling rose-petals showered around us like red snow.

He dropped the cape, revealing the garb of a kilted highlander in battle-ready dress beneath. We clapped and yelled in appreciation as he drew a long sword from its scabbard and began a series of stylized, almost balletic, moves across the stage.

"I have come far to be here with you, my brothers of old," he said. "From miles across the sea your pain and suffering has been heard. The rocks speak to their brethren, even as you hew and cut. You are not alone. Scotsmen are *never* alone. Not when we have the auld tunes."

The fiddle started up again in the distance, fluttery, like a little bird in flight.

Another collective sigh ran through us, like wind in a field of wheat. The Scotsman smiled and spoke over it, his voice low but carrying over the crowd.

"I promised to heal what ails you. And I will keep to that oath. But first, in the grand tradition, we will have a volunteer from the audience."

Malone stepped forward. I was looking straight at him at the time, and it looked like he had moved before even thinking about it. A momentary confusion showed in his face, but his features were grim and set hard as he stepped onto the stage.

"See," the Scotsman said. "A volunteer, at the first time of asking. What would you have me do with him? Shall I cut him in half?"

He raised the sword and made a mock swing, stopping just short of Malone's ample belly. As one the crowd cheered. That did not improve Malone's mood. He looked fit to burst as he turned to the Scotsman.

"What is your purpose here?" he said, his voice high, almost a shout.

The Scotsman merely smiled. "I have already said. I have come from the auld Homeland, come to heal what ails these good people."

He swung the sword in the air above his head. The Irishman flinched, but when the Scotsman's hands came down he had the fiddle in one hand and a bow in the other. He put it to his chin and started to play, the tune coming from the far distance at first, but getting closer, ever louder. The ground beneath us seemed to swell and *thrum.* As one, we began to sway.

A loud Irish voice broke the spell.

"Enough of this mummery."

He made to reach for the fiddle but the Scotsman danced away, still playing, mocking Malone and teasing him by throwing notes and phrases full in the Irishman's face. The tent seemed to melt and flow and we danced in time, lost in a place where there was no hurt, no tiredness, only blessed peace.

We were dropped back into grim reality by the blast of a single gunshot. The fiddle blew apart in a cloud of splinters, and a red hole appeared at the Scotsman's neck. He was dead before he hit the ground. Malone stood over him, his Colt still smoking in his hand.

I do believe the crowd might have lynched Malone that very night had he not held such clout over us that we depended on him for almost everything from employment to food. As it was the tent was in uproar until he fired another shot over our heads.

"Go home," he shouted. "All of you. And I want you all at work as usual on the morrow."

We went, with the sound of the gunshot ringing in our ears.

For the rest of the evening I thought of little but the sound of the fiddle and the tune that had seemed both so strange yet so familiar. The air played in my head even after I lay down abed. So when I heard the strain of a fiddle starting up, I was unsure for long seconds whether I was awake or asleep.

But this was no pastoral tune. Yes, it spoke of the auld country, but now it held a martial air that spoke of battles against tyranny, of blood feuds and scores settled. The auld country called... and we answered.

When I walked out into the street I found all of my neighbours already there. We followed the sound of the fiddle, dancing to its tune all the way to the small cemetery at the rear of the church.

As we shuffled into the hallowed ground the tune finally faltered and fell silent. I was first on the scene, which is why it has fallen on me to relate this tale. The sight I saw will be forever etched on my memory.

It was obvious that Malone had started to dig an unmarked grave for his *victim*. A shovel sat on the ground beside a pile of disturbed earth. Two bodies lay there. The Scotsman was still just as dead, the red hole gaping at his neck. But he had a broad smile on his face.

The reason for the smile was also obvious.

The mine-owner Malone lay beside him, a black tongue lolling from a wet mouth. He had been garrotted... almost beheaded.

Two fiddle strings were wrapped tight around his neck.

The Toughest Mile

-The First Mile -

He felt joy in the kill for the first time since his capture.

The gathered crowd roared as he struck the bear through the throat with a backhand swipe of the short sword. Blood sprayed over the nearest spectators, sending them into a braying frenzy. Garn scarcely noticed. He had already turned to the high podium where the witch sat, green eyes studying him coldly. Her bitches were grouped at her feet, all ten feigning disinterest. He knew from long experience that if he took one step closer, they would be at his throat before he could swing his blade.

Garn showed the witch the bloody sword, then threw it to the ground at his feet. He raised his hands high and the crowd cheered. After three years of fighting in the Pit, he had won his right to the challenge.

The Witch Queen did not seem happy at the outcome, but the law was indisputable: *If you can survive one hundred duels, you will have a chance to walk free, no longer a thrall. Merely pass the challenge.* Garn was the first in many years to survive long enough to take advantage of the offer. It had always been the thing foremost in his mind, even as he left his dead – man and beast alike – in a bloody wake on the sand of the Pit. It had not come without cost. In only his third fight he lost the smallest two fingers of his left hand to a wolf. In his sixtieth fight a fire-salamander had seared a burn that bit to his thighbone and brought a dull ache every cold night. And the bear, the last opponent thrown at him, had nearly got him. He'd only just managed to duck a swipe from a huge paw that would have taken his head off. The beast's claws only grazed him, leaving two bloody ridges across his scalp.

He'd ridden his luck many times, driven by the vision he held in his head of home, a dear green place far from the heat and sand of the pits. It had sustained him through many a dark night: the shutters rattle loudly against the window frame, and from the docks of Aer beyond he can hear rigging rattle and masts creak. The wind is an autumn southerly, whistling in over the Sleeping God's Pizzle, bringing with it the tang of salt spray and the faint but unmistakable stench of decaying whale meat. The ale is warm, and the woman on his lap is buxom.

He blinked, cleared his head.

That is the prize. First I must earn it.

He stood before the queen of this desert land and demanded his right – *the prize*.

Look at those eyes. She would kill me herself. But she is the Law. She has to give me my chance. To naysay me would be to deny her own authority.

He said nothing, merely stared back at her. The crowd slowly fell quiet, aware of the tension between their queen and their hero. He grabbed at the black, iron torc around his neck – the symbol of his servitude.

It is time for this to be removed.

He didn't have to say it. She knew only too well what he desired most in life. She nodded and waved a hand. The heavy metal ring broke in two pieces that fell to the sand with a double *thud*. The crowd cheered and whooped. The witch looked like she had swallowed a fly. Garn smiled.

She will miss me – both for the spectacle in the Pit – and mayhap more for the nights in her bed.

He could have killed her many times on those nights when she sent for him, but he had submitted, knowing that he would be hunted all his life if he gave in to the urge. There was only one way to freedom.

And now I have a chance.

Besides, there were far worse places to spend a desert night than in the arms of a green-eyed witch who knew how to please a man. He had enjoyed those nights, looking forward to them with anticipation, even though he could never admit it, to her or to himself.

She looked down at him, and he heard her, in his mind, whispering.

"There is no need to run. Come to my bed. Sleep, and I will take you into my arms forever."

But the vision he had carried these long years was too strong, the call of the cold tavern with warm ale too alluring. He shook his head and stood his ground.

"So be it. But I shall ask again. Think on it."

She turned and addressed the crowd.

"Bring him food and water," the Witch Queen said. "And prepare the *Corridor.* The challenge will begin in two hours."

There was one final cheer, somewhat muted as the crowd jostled for position to leave the arena, eager for the choicest seats for the spectacle to come. Garn sat down in the dust and drying blood of the killing ground and dreamed of home until his meal – one way or another, the last he would eat as a Pit fighter – was brought to him. The salted pork was succulent, the water clean and pure, and when the allotted time came round he felt strong again, in body and in will. When he stood he thought he had been left alone in the small amphitheatre that surrounded the fighting pit, but once again he felt the tickle in his mind, and heard her soft voice.

"Come to my bed. Sleep, and I will take you into my arms forever."

He looked up at the throne. She was still there, but the bitches were gone to wait for him in the place beyond. The witch nodded once and waved a hand. There was a grating of metal on stone and the massive iron gate immediately beneath her throne opened with a squeal that echoed round the empty amphitheatre.

Garn stood and lowered his gaze to view what lay beyond the opened gate. From his vantage it looked like a long tunnel with the sun showing at the far end. But he knew it was a trick of the light. It was a corridor, built so long ago than no one in Jonta knew its provenance, but only that it was ten miles long, lined on both sides with tall banks of seats where spectators could watch the pursuit. Vendors would already be selling bread, wine and Janax tea to the gathering throng who were about to see something that only happened once or twice in a lifetime. A gladiator was going to run the corridor; and from the growing clamour and raised voices drifting through from beyond, it sounded like the whole city had come to see him.

"There is still time," she said, aloud this time, though barely above a whisper. "Climb up here with me and we can be off. I have new pleasures to show you."

Garn didn't look away from the view through the gate. He could not look her in the eye for fear of losing even a fraction of his resolve.

She saw that he was resolute.

"I wish you luck," the witch said. "But I fear my bitches will be feasting well tonight. I shall miss you in my bed."

Garn smiled, but still did not look at her.

"I shall dock their tails and bring each to you," he replied and widened his grin.

She turned and left, leaving Garn alone in the auditorium. He'd dreamed of this moment, often wondering what he would feel. In truth, all he felt was eagerness and anticipation; he wasn't about to let this chance slip away. But first he divested himself of his armour. It was needed against the heavier weapons used in the Pit, but would only weigh him down on the chase. He eyed the bloody sword on the ground, but he'd been told the rules often enough.

The runner cannot bring weapons into the corridor – only his wits.

Clad only in a cotton shirt, his leather kilt and soft sandals, he walked through the gate and into a wall of noise. As soon as he made his appearance the chant went up – his name, shouted out by thousands, as it had been for months now, getting steadily louder as he approached this day, this destiny. He raised a hand in acknowledgement and the noise went up to an ever-higher level. Firebrands were already lit along the length of the run, a twin line of flame showing him the way to his freedom.

And the bitches, desert women bred to run, were already in their positions, waiting. They had swapped their silks and damasks for supple leather and soft boots, and they stared at him as if he might be lunch. They had all tied their waist-long hair in long braids that draped around their shoulders like black snakes. Garn had never been swayed by their pretence at softness, so their attempts at intimidation did not reach him at all. He'd known all along the witch's assassins... bodyguards... whatever she liked to call them, were little more than trained animals in women's skin. Bred mute, bred for speed, bred for running.

And Garn was to be the quarry.

The crowd went quiet as the Witch Queen moved through from above the fighting pit to take her place in the throne room above the main gate. She spoke, seemingly only a whisper, but Garn knew that even those making their way to the far reaches of the corridor would hear her. He tuned her out, focused on building his own mental fortitude – he'd need it before this evening was much older. Besides, she was reciting the rules and he knew all that he needed to know about them. One chaser would be released to chase him every turn of the small hourglass by the Witch Queen's hand, and if he got to the end of the ten miles in one piece, he would be a free man.

She said *if...* in his head he heard *when*.

The chaser at the head of the line held a long *flensing* in her left hand. She licked it, raising blood from her tongue, and smiled from a mouth that dripped red.

Garn turned his back on her. When a gong sounded he broke into a loping run. He had no strategy beyond running and killing. The bitches might have been bred for this purpose...

But so was I.

The crowd bayed and roared. After a time he heard the ringing of a gong. A chaser was on the way. A few minutes later he reached the marker that denoted he had reached the end of the first mile.

-The Second Mile -

He was going to have to look back, to check on the proximity of his first pursuer.

But not yet. Why waste energy? The crowd will let me know when they are close.

He was starting to work up a sweat despite the rapidly cooling night air. The wound in his scalp throbbed and burned in time with the thud of his heartbeat in his ears. The noise wasn't quite loud enough to drown out the gong denoting that the second chaser was on her way.

He pushed onward, fighting the urge to up the pace, trying to maintain the same steady lope that had always served him well on the deer hunts of his youth. Just the memory of home gave him a fresh burst of energy. He could see the marker for the end of the second mile. It was still some ways ahead of him, but he was getting there.

The roar of the crowd suddenly increased to a crescendo, and he knew the first chaser was almost upon him. He turned sharply on his left heel and dropped into a fighter's crouch. Just in time – she was only twenty yards away and coming fast, her braid swinging in rhythm with her paces.

Garn let her come. She feigned to go left, but he'd been watching her eyes. When she dodged right he was waiting. As her arm brought the flensing knife down he managed to block it at the wrist. He gave a single twist. The *crack* as the bone broke sounded loud even above the roar of the crowd. He used her weight against her, and as she followed through the knife slid easily between her ribs. She was dead long before she hit the ground.

Garn held on firmly to the knife, feeling it tug against bone as the bitch fell away. He took just enough time to take her braid off with one cut close to her scalp, turned and started to run. He tied the hair to his belt, and it hung behind him like a tail, dripping blood on the dry sand.

The gong sounded, more distant now. The third chaser was on her way. Shortly afterwards he passed the marker.

-The Third Mile -

He felt the new tail sway behind him and smiled, remembering his words to the witch. *I shall dock their tails and bring each to you.* He was off to a good start. He could not expect the others to be dispatched so easily – the first had been too eager, too ready to grab glory. In her haste she had underestimated Garn. But the others would now be more circumspect.

Which may also be to my advantage. It may buy me more time to build a lead.

The thrill of the first kill sustained him for almost

half a mile, but the sound of the next gong, almost inaudible over the roar of the crowd, surprised him. He had thought to be closer to the next marker before then. He risked a look over his shoulder. The second chaser was coming on fast, some way behind but moving much faster than Garn. Once again he considered turning and waiting, but he could see even through the ever deepening darkness that the third pursuer was also in view, moving like a big cat full-pelt on the hunt.

He started to put more effort into it, trying to maintain a lead. Up until now he had managed to ignore the presence of the crowd, his focus all on the task at hand. But when he felt a sting at his shoulder and put his hand there, he felt fresh blood and heard a *thud* in the sand behind him. He had no time to stop and look but felt sure it had been a small knife of some sort. A second projectile hit him in the thigh and stuck there for a second before falling to the ground. Garn turned, just in time to see a heavy-set man in the crowd raise an arm for a third throw. The man smiled broadly as he saw Garn looking.

"Run little pig!" the man shouted, and threw a small, thick-bladed knife.

Barely having to break step, Garn plucked the missile out of the air and in the same movement sent it straight back to embed itself in the man's neck. The tormentor fell, gurgling, and a wash of blood ran down his chest.

"Die little pig!" Garn shouted, laughing as he ran past.

The crowd roared even louder.

Garn's breath started to come heavier. His throat felt

dry and dusty, scraped and scoured by sand. He risked another look over his shoulder. The second chaser was closing in on him; the third a mere spot in the distance at the moment, but even from this far he could see she was gaining fast.

I must stand, for a time. If I run too far, too fast, I won't be fit to fight, and they will just drag me down.

He veered to one side of the corridor. A huge portion of the crowd surged forward, arms outstretched, eager to touch him..

"Wine," he shouted, "A drink for a thirsty man."

Someone thrust a deerskin at him. He sucked at it eagerly. The wine was vinegar-sour but it wetted his throat and put fire in his belly. As he took a second gulp, the crowd screamed, alerting him to danger. He ducked and turned in one movement.

The second chaser had thrown a long knife, hoping to catch him in the back. Garn thought he felt it pass through his hair. There was a pained *grunt* behind him – some unfortunate in the crowd got more excitement than he had bargained for. Garn had no time to check. The chaser had used up the weapon she was allowed – but she was also allowed to use anything found in her path. That included the small throwing knife that had fallen after scoring Garn's thigh. Still running she bent, picked up the blade, and rushed on, an eager grin on her face.

Garn waited until she got almost at arm's length. As she raised the knife, aiming for his eyes, he blew a mouthful of wine in her face...

... and gutted her with the flensing knife as she blinked.

The next pursuer was close now. It was now too dark to see any of the others, and Garn knew he was almost too far away to hear the gong, but he had to assume that at some point soon all the bitches would be on the hunt.

Let them come. I am ready.

He took a calculated risk and stood his ground, waiting for the third. The crowd bayed for blood. They got it soon enough.

The chaser had no guile to her. She came straight on, mouth open in a soundless scream. Garn plucked her out of the air like a doll and broke her back across his knee with about as much effort as he would have made breaking a twig.

He left her there, broken and wondering what had just happened. When he started running again he had three tails hanging from his belt.

He passed the next marker grinning widely.

-The Fourth Mile -

He began to hope. The first three bitches had gone down far easier than expected; he had already delivered a blow to the witch's authority. And the crowd loved him for it. They chanted his name in time with his every step as he fell once more into a steady loping stride. The wine felt like acid in his stomach and he started to sweat again almost immediately, but he had his focus back. He set his eyes on the alley of flaming brands stretching out ahead of him and ran towards his freedom.

The braids of hair swung behind him. He knew this was a piece of vanity on his part, something that his old instructor would have berated him for.

Never take anything into the arena that you do not need for the fight.

But he did need the braids – or rather he would, when he reached the end, when he faced the witch a free man with the ten braids to lay in front of her. The thought of her face at that moment gave him more than enough reason to leave the hair where it was, tied to his belt and swaying gently with each pace.

It was almost full dark now, the flaming brands throwing flickering shadows on the sand before him. He listened intently as he ran, waiting for a signal from the crowd that the next chaser was closing in.

It never came.

He approached the next marker.

She should have caught me by now.

He saw the reason when he took a look back. Not one but two chasers ran side by side some way behind him.

And they are not gaining.

They kept pace with him, and he saw their tactic – they would wait for a third, and maybe even a fourth, to join them before closing up. They had noted how easily their sisters had fallen.

Their next attack would be a co-ordinated one.

-The Fifth Mile -

He stopped and turned.

Better to face two than three or four.

But he wasn't going to be given the chance. The pursuers stopped thirty paces away and stood still. Garn started running – towards the chasers. They retreated before him and behind them he saw another closing up fast.

They are trying to lure me. I am wasting precious time here.

He turned his attention back to his eventual goal, set his mind on the target, and ran. Once again the crowd took up the chant and he used the rhythm to set his pace. He ran, giving no thought to his pursuers, only thinking of the end of the corridor and his freedom. By the time he reached the next marker and looked back there were three of them a hundred yards behind and keeping pace.

The attack will come soon.

-The Sixth Mile -

As before, the crowd told him first. They chanted his name with every step, and when the noise changed to a shapeless roar he knew it was time. He turned to see three chasers, closing fast. He refused to wait for them to come to him. He ran, heading straight for them.

The left-side chaser helped Garn's cause by stumbling, seeming confused by his decision. She lost her footing and fell sideward, disturbing the balance of the chaser beside her.

Garn concentrated on the third chaser to his right. She showed Garn her knife as he moved in. She slashed and Garn parried, aware already that he was the superior knife-fighter. He feinted to go under the bitch's knife, then twisted his wrist and went over. The steel felt like an extension of his arm as it slid through her throat and, with a twitch of the wrist, sliced the jugular vein and sent her gurgling to the ground.

He sensed a movement to his left, and turned and ducked in one movement as a knife flashed in front of him. He felt a sting in his shoulder and blood flowed. The second chaser advanced, knife swinging wildly. Again, this one was no knife fighter, but she was strong and fast, her heavy blade sending shocks up Garn's arm every time he had to parry.

The third chaser had regained her composure and moved in to join the fight.

I have to finish this fast.

Garn stepped inside the swing of the closest attacker, cramping her movements and at the same time smashing the pommel of the flensing knife into her face, feeling her nose crush wetly with the force of the blow. She let out a yell, but managed to push Garn away, and came back at him, knife swinging.

He let her come, and, just as the knife seemed set to slash at his throat, he stepped to one side. The momentum of her swing carried her forward and off balance. Garn thrust his blade deep between her ribs, at the same time kicking her to the sand. A final kick to the side of her head put her out of the fight.

Garn had no time to think. The third had advanced, snarling like a cornered wildcat. This one carried herself like a true knife-fighter... she wasn't about to rush in swinging. Garn circled her, saying nothing, trying to stay calm.

She sent her blade out in a quicksilver flicker that he only just managed to parry as it was over his heart. It slid off a rib, bringing a flare of pain. He felt more blood flow, wet heat at his side. He stepped forward into a lunge that caught her off guard, but she managed to weave to one side and Garn's stroke cut a slice across her ribs instead of taking her through the heart. She let out a yell and stepped into the attack with renewed vigor. Garn was hard pressed to defend himself.

The sound of clashing steel echoed around them as they circled, searching for an opening. Blood flowed freely at his side.

The wound is deeper than I thought. I must finish this.

He decided to try a risky feint, one that he sometimes had success with on the training ground. He stepped backwards, as if retreating before her attack, and let his right leg give under him, feigning a stumble and letting his knife hand go down towards the sand, looking as if he was going to use it to steady himself. As he hoped, she went for his suddenly exposed left-hand side. He ignored the descending blade, and, with a straight arm, punched the knife upwards, catching her under the ribs, pushing through to cleave her heart.

She fell, already a dead weight, pinning Garn to the sand, and he had to use all his remaining strength to push the body off and stand upright. Suddenly the crowd fell quiet and all he heard was his own heavy panting.

As he cut the chasers' braids he looked back down the corridor. There was another chaser just in sight, but he had enough time to collect his prizes. He tied the braids to his belt and took stock. He had a small wound on his shoulder, little more than a scratch, but the one at his side was more serious. It still bled, and when he prodded his finger at the hole it flared in white-hot pain.

I cannot run with the wound bleeding like this.

He walked over to the nearest firebrand and lifted it from its slot.

The crowd roared in approval as he rolled the brand in the sand then touched the still glowing tip to the wound, cauterising the site. He smelled burned hair and flesh. When he touched the area, there was no sign of blood. The pain was excruciating, but he knew how to handle that. He pushed it away until it was a ball in a far corner of his mind. It shouted for attention as he started to move and shouted louder as he broke into a run. But his instructor had taught him well.

Pain is inevitable. Suffering is optional.

He was moving as well as ever as he passed the marker.

-The Seventh Mile -

He thought he was strong, in mind and body. But despite his wounds it was his thoughts that started to betray him now. His instructor would have him focus on nothing but the goal, all else subservient to that one thought. But despite himself, Garn could not escape the witch in his mind – her soft yet hard body, those green eyes in which it was possible to get lost for an age and forget the trials of the pit. The thought that he might never again share the royal bed brought regret.

And with that regret, his mind betrayed his body. Barely midway between the markers he felt the first sign of the draining tiredness of fatigue. He started to plod, as if treading through water, and each step became a greater burden. The crowd sensed him weakening and took to chanting his name with increased fervour. The sound rang in his ears, echoing the length of the corridor. Garn tried to take heart from it, in the same way as he had used the crowd to his advantage during his many fights in the pit, but it got harder with every step.

I cannot go on like this. I will be run down like a wounded deer.

Indeed, he was starting to feel like an old stag; his defiance was the only thing keeping him upright in the face of an implacable foe armed with more speed and superior weaponry. And with that came a memory of cornering a huge buck, of his brother Finn rushing forward – only to be impaled on the antlers of a resurgent beast.

I must use the cunning I learned that night.

He slowed, first to a walk, then stumbling, almost falling. He made a show of dropping to one knee. The crowd groaned, but Garn took the opportunity for a look behind him. The chaser was thirty paces behind, and showing no signs of hanging back.

This one wants the kill for herself. That shall be her undoing.

Garn made to stand, but fell into another stumble, leaving his back exposed and risking everything to his reflexes. The chaser leapt, the crowd roared, and Garn spun, the knife coming up to where the bitch's rib cage should have been waiting. But this one had wiles of her own. His knife caught her arm and sliced a deep wound there, but in the same movement she had fallen to the ground, rolled, and cut a groove across the back of his left leg, a hair's-breadth away from hamstringing him completely. His leg gave way beneath him and he fell heavily, trying to roll aside, but not fast enough. Her blade bit deep again, this time taking him through the muscle of his left bicep. Before she could withdraw the knife he rolled further away, attempting to drag the weapon from her grasp while it was still embedded in his arm. But she proved tenacious, rolling with his pull and punching him so hard on the side of his head that his vision started to go. Instead of going with the blow Garn grabbed her arm, pulling her towards him. He slammed his forehead into her face, cracking against her nose, and she fell to one side. Once more he rolled, this time pressing his weight on top of her, pinning her to the sand.

She spat a glob of blood in his face and tried to chew at his cheek. He head-butted her again, twice for good measure. She stayed down as he strangled her with her own braid.

He was gentle with her when he cut her pleat, and he said a prayer to the Gods as he attached it to his kilt.

She was brave. Give her a place at the table. I would see her again.

The roar of the crowd was the loudest yet as he stood and looked back down the corridor. Two of the last three chasers stood thirty paces away, watching him keenly. He tested his weight on his left leg. He could stand, maybe even walk, for a time, but there would be no more running. He flexed his injured bicep and got a flash of pain, but nothing that would stop him using the arm if he needed to.

I am alive, I have weapons, and three miles to go. I

will have my freedom.

He turned his back on the chasers and started to walk, limping at first, then with more stability as he gained confidence that his leg would not fold beneath him. He passed the next marker with his name echoing along the length of the corridor.

-The Eighth Mile -

He walked the full mile, getting ever slower as his wounds started to tell and his fatigue grew ever deeper. The chasers, three of them together now, followed twenty paces behind.

Garn smiled.

Almost there.

-The Ninth Mile -

As he passed the second to last marker the chasers moved up to take closer order, keeping ten paces behind him. He paid them no mind. Either they attacked or they didn't. Either way, he was prepared.

Now we draw near to it. I will bide my time, and let them decide.

Sitting quietly, doing nothing, spring comes, and the grass grows by itself.

He had been staring at his feet for some time, concentrating on putting one foot in front of the other. His mind was far away, in the cold dockside bar in Aer in winter, with a snell wind whistling over the Sleeping God's Pizzle, a tankard of warm mead in his right hand and a wench in his lap.

Even in that well played dream the girl had green eyes.

His various wounds burned fiercely. He had lost blood – not too much to disable him, not yet, but he was a far weaker man than he had been at the start of this journey. Looking up, he saw a brighter flame at the end of the corridor – the marker for the finish.

She will be there, waiting. Those green eyes will be watching for me to come to her. I will not disappoint the witch.

He summoned up the last of his energy and broke into a stumbling run.

The crowd roared his name.

The chasers followed.

-The Tenth Mile -

He was less than four hundred yards from the flame when he fell. He'd been right; the witch was there, waiting. He did not have to see those green eyes to feel their gaze on him, to lose himself in their depths.

Rest, the eyes said. *Sleep, and I will take you into my arms forever.*

His legs gave way and he tumbled to the ground. His eyes started to droop closed.

The chasers moved in.

But a fighter's instinct was not so easily quenched. They thought him down and came on in a line, the fastest first. That was their undoing. Still lying flat on the ground he swung out a foot and swept the legs from the first. She fell beside him and he planted the flensing knife in her throat before she knew what had happened.

The second aimed a thrust at his eyes. He kicked her in the middle, the shock running through his whole body.

Before he could follow through, the third was on him. He rolled away just in time to avoid a thrust that would have skewered him. He took another risk, throwing the flensing knife – his main weapon – at the third attacker. He was already moving, not waiting to see the result. The one he'd kicked was trying to rise. He kicked her again and stepped on her throat, crushing her larynx and breaking her neck with one stomp.

One to go.

He turned towards where the third attacker should be.

She sat on her knees, the flensing knife protruding from her left eye, the other staring at the dead lands beyond.

I am free.

He had one more task before finishing. He took the braids of the downed women and, untying the others from his belt, he staggered across the last yards that separated him from his prize.

-The Toughest Mile -

She was waiting for him beside the flame that marked the end of the challenge, in front of a massive wooden gate. She looked him up and down. The crowd fell quiet. The only sound was the crackle of firebrands and the heavy rasp of Garn's laboured breathing.

"Was it worth it?" she said softly.

He said nothing, merely dropped the ten bloody braids at her feet.

She lowered her voice to a whisper so that only he could hear. *"Sleep and I will take you into my arms forever."*

His gaze never left her eyes as he spoke.

"There is a cold tavern on a far dock that has a flagon of warm mead and a warmer-still wench waiting for me. She has been waiting too long."

He smiled coldly when he saw the anger flare in her eyes, all joy tempered by a sadness in his own heart at having done it. But his freedom was close now. He must not waver.

He looked her in the eye, daring her to refuse him.

She sighed, waved a hand, and the gate opened. The crowd chanted his name in time with his paces as Garn walked out of the corridor, a free man.

It was a mile to the edge of the city, and the whole way he thought of nothing but her deep green eyes.

The Havenhome

Taken from the personal journal of Captain John Fraser, Captain of the Havenhome, a cargo vessel. Entry date 16th October 1605.

My dearest Lizzie.

Today has been the worst day of my life. As I sit here, warm in my cabin, whisky at hand, I can scarcely believe the deprivations suffered by the brave people of this far flung outpost. I should have stayed at home like you asked. You would have kept me warm. If only I'd done as you asked, then I might have been spared the terrible sights that met us at landfall.

We had no thought of winter when we left home port. Do you remember? It was a bright Scottish summer's day. You cried as we parted, and the sun made rainbows of your tears. I can still see you now, standing on the dock, waving us off. How I wish I could look at you, just one more time, one more time to warm my heart against the cold that has gripped us all.

After the auspices of its beginning, our voyage soon reminded us that the sea is not always benign. After four months at sea my crew expected some ease from the biting winds and cold autumnal spray, some shelter from the elements that had assailed them so assiduously. And some were expecting something more, having heard tell of the harbour tavern of our destination, and the warm doxies who waited there.

Cold comfort was all they found.

We arrived under a slate grey sky, having to tack

hard against a strong offshore wind that faded and died as soon as we entered the safe haven of the natural harbour. I thought it passing strange that there was no-one on the dockside to mark our arrival. We have been looked for these past two months, and the Havenhome is tall enough to be seen from many a mile. And yet no smoke rose from the colony, despite the chill in the air and the ever-present autumnal dampness. There was already a pall over my heart as we hove to.

"Mayhap there is a town meeting," the pastor said as we stood at the prow.

"Aye, mayhap," I said. But my heart did not believe it. I knew already there was some dark power at large. Perhaps I do have a touch of the Highlander sight after all.

Jim Crawford was ashore before anyone else, running down the dock.

The First Mate called after him.

"Do not tire the doxies out, Master Crawford."

"I will have first choice," the deck hand shouted, laughing. "I'll leave you the ugly ones. But if you want any ale, you'd best be quick, for I have a terrible thirst."

We found him again when we disembarked and headed into town. He was first at one thing... he'd been right at that... he was first, but by no means last, to fall in a dead faint.

At our last visit some three years ago this was a thriving town of a hundred souls, living off the land that God gave them, and maintaining peaceful trading relations with the natives. There had even been talk of expansion, with land to the south earmarked for a church.

Now it will only be used as a cemetery, for they are dead... every last soul of them.

The fortifications have not been breached and there is no evidence of a fight. There were just the bodies of the dead, as if the Lord decided in that instant to take them to their heavenly rest. They lay, scattered on the ground like fallen leaves, faces grey, ashen and almost blue. They are cold to the touch, their eyes solid and milky, like glass marbles sunk in a ball of snow.

It was all the First Mate and I could do to keep the men from fleeing. Some did indeed fall to their knees in prayer and supplication.

"What could have caused this, Cap'n?" the First Mate asked.

"Mayhap t'was a freak storm," Coyle the cook said. "For surely we have seen the same thing happen to a man at the mast in the far north waters?"

"But these are not the north waters," the pastor replied. "This land is most clement, even in comparison to our own home. Men do not freeze in October. This is the devil's work, mark my words."

As for myself, I kept my peace then, but as I saw more of what lay on the streets I came to think they might both have been right.

I was in the court house, standing over the still, dead bodies of Josiah MacLeod and his family and trying not to weep when the pastor made his final report.

"We have searched the whole town, Captain. As far as we can tell the entire population has been felled, for no one answered our calls, although our entreaties have been long and loud. God rest their souls."

The burials began.

The small ones were the worst. The sun had partially thawed their bodies, but when you lift them you feel the hard frozen core inside. It is all that you can do to keep from weeping as you lay them into the too-small holes.

After the burials were finally complete our pastor called for a service of remembrance, but I knew the mood of the crew better. I had the cook break open our cargo and prepare a feast while I myself ensured that the tavern was made ready. The men had made a fair pass at clearing up the stench and gore of the carnage that had been wrought there. I was able to hide the last stains of blood with the judicious application of straw and wood chippings. What I couldn't mask was the memory; of the sightless eyes and the strewn limbs that had so recently laid scattered on the floor. I could only hope that a flagon of grog and the hearty company of my shipmates would dispel the chill that had fallen on my heart.

We set a great fire roaring in the hearth, cracked open what barrels we could find. We set to feasting and drinking with a gusto that only men far from home and long at sea will understand. Any guilt we might have felt at such merriment in a place where so much destruction had been wrought was quickly assuaged by the warmth of the fire and the sweet tang of the ale.

The evening began in fine fashion. The chef excelled even his own high standards. He managed to turn a few stone of potatoes, a leg of salted pork and some rough vegetables into a mouth-watering feast for each of us. Ale flowed freely. For a while we were almost warm.

The pastor recited 'The Lay of Lady Jane,' as bawdy a verse as any old sea-dog might muster. It was all the better coming from such an austere man of the cloth. Jim Crawford told a tall tale, of a man from Orkney who was twelve feet high with a two foot cock which he used to beat off foreign raiders. The room was filled with laughter.

"A tune from Stumpy Jack," came the call. When the eldest of the crewmen started on the squeeze box we could almost believe ourselves at home port once more. All went quiet as he started up that tune we all knew well, for we had sung it many times afore, albeit with lighter hearts and warmer circumstances.

Once more we sail with a northerly gale
Through the ice and sleet and rain.
And them coconut fronds in them tropic lands
We soon shall see again.
Six hellish months we've passed away
Sailing the Greenland seas,
And now we're bound from the arctic ground,
Rolling down to old Maui.

Stumpy Jack was old, but his voice was as clear and true as a young man's. It rang through the rafters, promising of hot sun and even warmer women. We all joined in on the chorus

Rolling down to old Maui, my boys,
Rolling down to old Maui.
We're southward bound from the arctic ground
Rolling home to old Maui.

Bald Tom found a tavern wenches' skirt. There was

much bawdy laughter as he moved among the tables pretending to be a doxie. If the talking and laughter was somewhat muted, and if some drank more than was good for them, we pretended not to notice. The Ulsterman told of his exploits against the Turks in Vienna, Bald Tom, still wearing the wenches' skirts, regaled us with tall tales of the Amsterdam brothels. Stumpy Jack sang the old whaler's songs before starting up that old sailor's favourite, "The Girl from Brest." We sang along at the top of our voices. The tavern rang loud, keeping the cold at bay, for a while at least. For that short span, we made a common bond that life was good once more. It nearly was.

By the time things went bad most of the crew were too far into their cups to notice.

"Bald Tom went out to the privy some ten minutes ago. He has been gone too long," the First Mate said to me.

"Tis not unknown for him to linger over a shit," I replied.

"Aye, sir," the First Mate said, "but even for Tom this is too long. Especially when there is free ale and meat on the table."

He had it right. Bald Tom often loitered over his ablutions. He was teased mightily over it, but this was over-long, even for him. The pastor and I, being the two men least addled by the drink, went out into the night in search of him.

The cold was like a wall, hitting us square in our faces and taking our very breath.

"Let us leave him to his business," I said. "Tis too cold to go looking for the steam from his doings."

In truth, it was not just the cold that had me trembling. I had the fear of the devil in me. The memory of the fire inside the tavern was fading fast.

But the pastor was made of far sterner stuff than I.

"Let us continue and look a little further. He may be in trouble," the pastor said. "And there is evil afoot tonight. I feel it in my bones."

"Then have at it man, but make it quick. Already the cold bites at my ankles. At the rate the men are drinking, there will be none left for our return."

He led the way round the corner of the tavern, tall and proud in his faith while I cowered, cowed, behind him like a whipped scoundrel. I am not sure if the pastor prayed, but I was surely calling on God's protection more than enough for both our souls.

Bald Tom will be on the privy for the rest of eternity. We found him in the shed, squatting over the rough hole in the ground, skirts pulled up around his waist. He was no more than a cold block of flesh; frozen solid in mid shit. Had the pastor not been there I believe I may have laughed... in jest at first, then later in hysteria.

"Lets us have him inside by the fire," the pastor said. "Mayhap he can yet be revived."

I nay-said him. "Leave him be. He is deader than anything I have ever clapped eyes on. Deader even than Jim McLean of Banchory, and he had his head taken off by a corsair."

The pastor stood over the body to say the words that would speed Bald Tom to paradise, but I had known the man well. I'm certain that the resting place of his soul would be more than warm enough to thaw any part of him that was yet frozen after the journey.

The pastor was taking over-long over the formalities, while all I could think about was the fire in the hearth, and a flagon of spiced rum. I was about to turn away when it suddenly got colder... colder even than the time the sea had frozen around us off Trinity Bay in Newfoundland and we'd been locked in place for a month with naught but salted fish to sustain us. Ice formed in my beard. It crackled to the touch. The last half-inch of my moustache came away in one piece in my palm.

We looked at each other, the pastor and I. I hope my own eyes held less abject fear than I saw in his, but I cannot guarantee it. "Have you finished telling the Lord of Bald Tom's piety?" I asked, speaking loudly, as if the very sound of my voice would keep the cold at bay.

"That I have, Captain," he replied. "But it is my own soul that concerns me at this moment."

"I have found that a flagon of spiced rum is good for most things that ail the soul," I replied.

"Then let us retire within, and you can show me," the pastor said. "For it is colder than fisher-wife's teats out here."

Outside the shed something moved, a shuffling, stumbling. Then came a moan, as of a man in pain.

The pastor instinctively moved to help and stepped outside.

"No," I called. I put out a hand.

He was dead before I could help him. He froze, stiff as a board in the wink of an eye. One cold eye stared up at me in amazement before it too froze, all sight going as life left him. He fell, solid as a stone, part in, part out of the privy door.

The sound of shuffling got louder. The cold cut deep, reaching my bones. I am ashamed to say it, but I was mightily afeard, struck immobile with terror as whatever manner of thing was beyond the door crept closer. The noise stopped just outside the shed door. Something pulled the pastor out of the shed, his body scraping on the ground like a slab being slid from a tomb.

I bent, thinking to take his arms, to try to counter whatever had him. But one touch of his bare hand was enough for the cold to burn my palm to the bone. Whatever had the pastor tugged at him again. The body was dragged away out of my sight. But not out of hearing.

My ears were assailed with cracking and crunching... teeth grating on icy flesh and bone. I could not tell you what manner of creature made such foul sounds, for I could not bring myself to look.

The sounds continued for some time while the cold crept ever deeper through me until finally I could take it no longer... I squeezed past Bald Tom and made an attack on the shed's rear wall.

The noises of feeding stopped. Behind me the privy door creaked as something pushed inside.

I renewed my attack on the wall, kicking and punching like a man possessed. The wall fell before me like dry kindling. There was a single moment of icy cold, a breath on the back of my neck that I will remember for whatever life I have left, then I was away and heading for the tavern as fast as my legs would take me.

~-o0O0o-~

Once I made my escape from the privy I was too afeard to risk a look backwards. If I had seen the pastor's fate I do believe I may have given up my soul to the Lord there and then. But all I could see in my mind was the roaring heat of the fire, a beacon calling me to safety. I was close enough to hear the crew singing:

"There was a young lady from Brest,
Who had an enormous chest
You could place a whole city
On each of her titties
And hide a small hill in her vest."

I mouthed along with the words. Although I was afraid to speak them aloud, the very nature of them, reminding me of home and the fireplace around the Inn on the harbour of a summer's evening, gave me what strength I needed to keep moving.

I had a bad moment when my feet slipped, and threatened to give way under me.

In my mind's eye I saw something reach for me, something foul and cold from the worst nightmare of my childhood. I felt its cold dead breath on my neck. I thought that my maker had finally called for me.

I do believe I screamed, alone there in the dark. I may have lain there, unable to move if I hadn't at the very moment thought of you, my dearest Lizzie. It was the memory of you on the dockside that got me moving. I managed to scramble away and I burst like a fury into the tavern.

Some of the crew turned and, on seeing me, laughed. But there must have been a fell look in my eyes, for their laughter died on their lips. The room fell suddenly quiet.

"What has happened, Cap'n," the First Mate called.

I had no time to answer. I turned and slammed the oak door behind me as soon as I was full inside, but even then I felt the cold seep through the wood to my hands.

"Stoke the fire," I called out.

No one moved. They were all stuck immobile by the shock of my sudden entrance.

I backed away from the door as a silver sheen of hoar frost ran across its surface.

"Where's the pastor? Where's Bald Tom?" the voices cried.

"Dead," I called out. "As you will be if you do not heed me. Stoke the fire! It is all that will save us now."

Young Isaac was having none of it. He was one of the ones who had helped clear out the tavern earlier; he'd seen at first hand the slaughter that had happened in this enclosed space.

"I'm not going to be taken like them others. If I'm to die, it will be out in the open," he called.

Before I could stop him he stepped forward and grabbed at the iron door handle... and was immediately frozen in place, icing-white like a grotesque cake decoration, mouth open in a mix of fear and surprise, his tongue lying like a cold grey stone in the floor of his mouth.

The men stood stock still, staring at what had become of the young deckhand.

"Stoke the bloody fire!" I called out once more. "Are you deaf as well as witless?"

The cold leeched through the door and started to reach for me. And still they didn't move.

"Have you forgotten those that we placed in the earth? Do you want to be like them? Stoke that bloody fire!"

Finally the First Mate had the sense to respond.

"You heard the Cap'n. Stoke this fire, or I'll throw you on alongside the logs."

Some of the men at last set to piling the hearthside logs on the fire while the rest of us backed slowly away from the door.

The wood, and young Isaac, were by now covered in a good half-inch of silver-grey ice, glistening red in the reflected firelight.

"Cap'n," Jim Crawford said fearfully. "What is it?"

"Death," I whispered. "As sure as eggs is eggs, 'tis death for us all, if we cannot get warm."

I heard the First Mate call out for more fuel, but I could not take my eyes from the encroaching edge of the ice.

The extent of it spread even as we watched, crawling along the walls as if laid down by some invisible painter, creeping across the floor towards our feet, tendrils reaching out, looking for prey.

As one man we stepped further backwards, each of us trying to get closer to the fire which roared at our backs but seemed to give out little heat. In truth I have never felt such cold, not even in the far north where the white bears roam. It was as if my very blood thickened in my veins.

A strange lethargy began to take me. I took a step forward, towards the door, then another. In my head I heard you, my dear Lizzie, calling me in from the field, calling me home for supper.

"Captain!" the First Mate cried. He pulled me back towards the fire, putting his own body between myself and the creeping ice.

"Best warm your hands," he said. "It's turned a bit on the nippy side."

I turned and faced the fire, feeling the heat tighten the skin across my cheeks. A layer of frost that had formed on my hands melted away. My blood began to move again so that I felt I might live, at least for a short time longer.

"Tell me, Cap'n," Stumpy Jack said. "Is it Old Nick himself come to take us? I always heard tell that fire was more in his line of work."

"I can't tell you that, Jack," I replied. "But there's more than just Mother Nature working agin' us this night. Stoke the fire, man. Keep stoking the fire. It's all that stands between us and a cold grave."

I helped Stumpy Jack load more wood on the flames. The fire had grown so as to fill the grate. We had to stand back and throw the fuel on, but still the ice crept across the room towards us and we were forced to huddle ever closer together.

"It's getting right cozy," Jim Crawford said. "When I dreamt of cuddling up with a warm body in this tavern, it wasn't any of you I had in mind."

"I don't know about that," someone called back. "Give me a shilling and I'll do for you. I'll even take me wooden teeth out."

That bought a round of laughter, and raised our spirits. But not for long.

One by one the men fell silent, each lost in his own thoughts.

There was naught to be heard but the crackle of the logs as the fire ate through fuel as fast as we could throw it on the flames.

The spread of the ice slowed.

Finally it stopped, a mere six inches from our feet. It did not retreat, but neither did it encroach any further. I began to believe that we might yet survive the night.

"Is it over, Cap'n?" the First Mate asked.

"Mayhap. Just pray it does not get any colder," I said. "And we may yet see the morning."

And then it came, the thing I had been dreading, the thing that had taken the pastor.

From outside we could hear shuffling, and a peculiar grunting, like a pig after truffles.

The wind outside rose, from nowhere to a howling, shrieking gale. Heavy sleet lashed like musket-shot against the shutters. The ice crawled once more, began to creep ever faster towards our feet.

"If you have any good ideas, Captain...?" the First Mate said.

"Truly, I can think of none, for what Christian man has ever endured such devilry?" I replied.

"Mayhap we should ask the Lord for some help?" the Mate said softly.

I asked myself what the pastor might do, were he still with us.

It took all of my strength, but I took myself further from the fire. I put my own body between the ice and my crewmen.

"Lads, we are in a dark place," I started. "I've led you into trouble aplenty afore now, and I've always brought you home safe. And so I will again. With a little help. The pastor has gone to join his Lord, but mayhap he'll turn back and lend us a hand if he hears us calling. Let us pray."

I led the men in the Paternoster. Their voices were strong and clear, but mine own faltered. I had been watching the ice.

Our appeals to our maker made not a jot of difference. The ice thickened, inexorably, throughout the room. It still crept slowly forward, and had almost reached all the way to the toe of my shoes.

In the end it was the practical things that helped most... we rotated the men round so that all would have a spell in front of the fire, but even that proved of little worth as the supply of logs dwindled and the fire burned down.

"Break up the trestles and tables lads," the Mate shouted. "Everything that's not breathing goes on the fire."

We burnt whatever we could find around us, from chairs and tables to the very leg of pork we had been eating earlier. The smell of cooking meat filled the tavern, but none of us were hungry.

We huddled together until you couldn't have squeezed a sheet of paper between us. In that way we kept ourselves alive.

But still the ice crept forward.

"Keep moving, men," the First Mate shouted. "Give everyone a sight of the fire."

The wind howled up a notch. The long night went on.

We shuffled in our tight huddle, looking forward only to our next spell in front of the fire, dreading our next pass in front of the door.

I came to believe there were voices in the wind, soft voices whispering hopes of peace and warmer climes if I would only close my eyes and allow myself to dream.

At other times I found myself talking to you, Lizzie, saying all the things I plan to say on my return, if I am spared long enough to see that day.

At some point in that long night we forgot to shuffle, each of us lost in our own icy hell. After a while no one stoked the fire. The ice crept ever closer.

"Goodbye, Jennie," I heard the First Mate whisper, which was passing strange, as his wife was named Charlotte. That was the last I heard. I fell into an icy black hole that had no bottom.

An eternity later I woke, from a dream of sun and hot sand into a nightmare of icy death.

At first I thought myself back in Aberdeen in my own bed, wrapped and swaddled in a thick quilt against a winter's morning.

Then I moved.

A cold blue hand fell onto my face.

It was no bed-sheet I lay under... it was the dead, frozen bodies of my crew. They had done their last duty to me, keeping me alive through the night.

I crawled, on hands and knees like a whipped dog, pushing myself through the blue dead forest of my crew-mates' limbs, promising the Lord that I'd be his faithful servant if he'd only but grant me one final glimpse of warm sun on green pastures.

The Lord finally heard me. I dragged my body clear and stood in front of the dying embers of the fire, tears blinding me as I surveyed the frozen bodies of my crew.

There came a moan from within the pile.

"Cap'n," the First Mate cried. "Are we in hell?"

I reached into the pile and found his warm hand. He dragged himself out as I used what paltry strength I had left to help his escape.

"Not in hell," I said as I lifted him to his feet. "But as close as mortal man should get."

More groans rose from the pile of frozen flesh. Of thirty men who entered the tavern the night before, only six of us pulled ourselves from the tangled pile and out into the near-forgotten warmth of a morning sun.

"Fuck me," Stumpy Jack said, squinting in the sudden light. "I ain't been in a pickle near as bad as that since John the Baker's Son insulted the Prince of Prussia's consort. I thought I was a goner for sure."

"We are all only here because of the Lord's mercy," the First Mate said. "Have heart boys. We may yet see hearth and home."

"And Jennie?" I said.

The First Mate smiled.

"Don't be telling the missus, Cap'n," he said. "Jennie is a widow in Liverpool... sort of a home from home, if you get my meaning?"

"Don't worry," Jim Crawford said. "We will ne'er get home again, so no one will ever know."

"Home again?" I said. "We may yet. But we must be strong if we are to survive another night such as the last one."

"As long as the sun shines, surely our strength will return," the First Mate said.

Indeed, the simple pleasure of the warmth of sunshine on my face was already pushing the memory of the cold away. I no longer felt that I might expire at any minute.

We stood, blinking, watching the ice and snow melt away with unnatural rapidity until all that was left was a dampness on the ground and the silent dead bodies of our brave shipmates back in the tavern.

And that was when we six made our vow.

"There will be no more hiding in locked taverns," I said to them. "We have lost too many friends and we will lose no more. We will make our stand on the Havenhome. And this time we will be ready."

~-o0O0o-~

At first the six of us who survived that hellish night in the tavern felt joy at the mere fact we were yet alive, with so many of our fellowship having fallen. Afterwards, the crew had a mind to up anchor and leave, never mind it would be near-nigh impossible for a crew of so few to get the vessel anywhere in open sea. In the end I shamed them into staying.

"I stay here," I shouted. "If you choose to go, you may leave me behind. Have you so far forgotten the fellowship we shared that you can leave your friends where they lie? Would you deny them the comfort of the words of the Lord?"

None spoke.

"And what of when we six are home and safe? What

will you tell their wives, their sweethearts? Would you be able to ever look them in the eye again? And when they ask in the taverns how it is that we six came home yet the others did not? Could you speak up and say that we ran like rats for the comfort of home while our shipmates lay dead in a tavern? I know that I could not. I will stay here, until we have eased the path to Paradise for our fallen."

"And I will stand with you, Cap'n, as always. You have led us through many dangers. I have trust that you will not betray us now."

The First Mate brought himself over to join me.

Together we stood there, while the remaining others stared at us sullenly, weighing their thoughts of mutiny against their loyalty to me, their captain.

In truth I myself wanted little more than to flee back to your soft arms, but I held firm, although I half expected at any moment for a storm to brew up and freeze me, immobile, to the spot. The storm did not come, but the last remainder of my crew did, eventually coming sheepishly to join us.

"The Lord will reward you, in this life or the next," I said to each of them.

"Do not be too quick with your praise, Cap'n," the First Mate said. "For mayhap they know as well as we do that four men, no matter how strong, could not even so much as get the boat out of this harbour, never mind across all the seas that separate us from home."

"Still, they have shown themselves brave enough to step down beside us. What each man holds in his heart lies between him and his maker, but their actions show them to be still true. For that, I give thanks."

"Then we will all give thanks together, to the Lord," the First Mate said. "The pastor may not be here, but that does not mean we should neglect our debts. Let us pray."

The First Mate led us in prayer, as solemn and faithful as if he himself was a pastor. Then Stumpy Jack started up the old songs. We sang "Wind and Sail, He Watches O'er Us," at the top of our voices.

I was the first to make my way back into that hellhole of the tavern, despite the heaviness that lay on my soul.

"Let us have at it, lads," the Mate said behind me, leading the rest inside. "We cannot have our friends lying here in the dark when there is warm sunshine to be had outside."

And so we lifted and we carried, trying not to remember the times we had spent with those who were now no more than cold meat under our hands. I will spare you the details, dearest Lizzie, but bringing the bodies of our fallen out of the tavern was a sore blow to our hearts. Some of us had a tear in our eye as we laid them in a row in front of the courthouse. But a far sorer blow was yet to come.

When we went to fetch the pastor and Bald Tom, neither of them was to be found.

I stood in the ruin of what was left of the privy.

I could find no sign that Bald Tom had ever been there, save for a single partially frozen shit on the ground.

Stumpy Jack wailed. "The devil has taken them. And it will be us for it next."

He would have fled there and then if the First Mate

hadn't held him by the scruff of the neck.

"Have courage, man," he said, loud enough for us all to hear. "Last night the Good Lord saved our sorry skins. He has a purpose for us all, even you, old Stumpy. All we have to do is trust him, and he will deliver us."

Those quiet words from the big man gave us all succour, but only until we dragged the bodies out to the cemetery.

None of us were prepared for the sight that met us.

This time old Stumpy did flee, screaming back to the boat as if all the demons of hell were after him.

The graves we had spent the last days digging all lay open, brown earth strewn every which way. The dead had not lain at rest, despite all the pastor's pleas and prayers. They had risen up, digging their way out of the cold earth.

There was no sign of any bodies, man, woman or child. Not a single one slept where we had put them.

"What shall we do, Cap'n? Shall we take them back to the Havenhome," the First Mate asked, but I had no answer.

"Leave them here," Jim Crawford shouted. "Leave them here. For if those we have said the words over can yet rise, then surely there is no hope for any of us."

"I must think on it," I said. "And I cannot hold a thought in my head while these graves lie before me. Leave our dead be. I will repair to my cabin. Mayhap the Lord will send me guidance."

We followed Stumpy Jack back to the boat; more slowly, but with no less trepidation in our hearts.

By the time we got back onto the Havenhome

Stumpy Jack was already blind drunk and no use to man nor beast.

"We have to go back and bury our crewmates," the First Mate said.

"Why bother. They will only be up and about again on the morrow," Stumpy Jack replied. He wept, a pitiful sight in such an old sea dog such as him.

"Jack has it right," Jim Crawford piped up. "Despite all our efforts, despite all the pastor's prayers, they've all come up again. And who is to know, mayhap the pastor and Bald Tom are with them even now."

Dave the Bosun's mate and Eye-Tie Frank stayed quiet. I saw they were already eyeing the grog. I allowed each man another half-cup.

"It's up to you, Cap'n," the First Mate said after swallowing a mouthful that would have floored a smaller man. "If you say we should go back and put them in the ground, then I'll make sure we all go as one."

May the Lord God forgive me; I left them there, lying out under the sun beside the empty graves.

"No," I replied. "Pull up the gangplank. We will spend this night on the Havenhome. I will sleep on it, and make a decision on the morrow."

But sleep was the furthest thing from my thoughts. I am ashamed to admit it, but I took to the grog, swilling it down as if the morrow did not matter, as if I had no responsibilities in the world. I know I promised you, dearest, but my solemn vow was not enough to keep me from it. I can only say in my own mitigation that I was far from hearth and home, and sore afeard. And if it is any consolation to you sweetest, I have no memory of the act, and I suffered the most fearful of headaches on awakening.

It was the First Mate who brought me out of my stupor.

At first I thought I had taken enough grog to blind me, but it was only that the sky outside had grown dark. Another night had fallen. There was a chill in the air.

"Cap'n. You need to see this," he said.

"Can't it wait?" I said, groaning as the result of my drinking gripped my head like a vise.

"Afraid not, Cap'n. If I left you asleep, you might never wake again."

"That might be no bad thing," I moaned.

He slapped me in the face, hard. I was so astonished I almost fell on my arse. I probably would have done had he not put out a hand to steady me.

"I'm rightful sorry, Cap'n, but your men need you sober and in charge. We are in perilous waters, and hard times. That is a mixture that requires a captain, not a drunken sot."

In all our time together he had never raised his voice to me before, let along strike me.

I was of a mood to be affronted, but one look at the fear in his eyes melted all passion away.

"You have the right, sir," I said to him. "If you see me lift another flagon of grog you can throw me in the brig and toss the key over the side."

"Best save your vow of abstinence for a bit," he said with a grim smile. "You might need a brew after you've seen what waits out on the dock."

He led me up on deck.

Moonlight shone down, illuminating the dock.

A single figure stood there, staring up at us.

It was our first sighting of an aboriginal, one that froze the very breath in my throat. He wore a headpiece of feathers that rose in a crown above his head and fell in a long tail down his back. His clothing looked to be animal skin roughly sewn together. His feet were bare.

But that wasn't what drew the eye. I had heard tell that the natives of these shores were red, almost the colour of blood, but this tall man was white as ivory, as cold as a stone. White eyes without a pupil stared up at us.

He raised his arms.

It snowed, out of that clear starry sky.

The First Mate looked past the native, down into the colony. "Dear Lord preserve us," he whispered.

I turned to follow his gaze.

The dead walked along the dock towards us, each of them staring with that white-eyed gaze. And there, at the front of the mob, stood a bulky man in a woman's skirt. Alongside him strode a tall grim-faced preacher dressed in black.

Bald Tom and the pastor had come back to visit their old shipmates.

~-o0O0o-~

The First Mate roused the remaining crew, all save Stumpy Jack who was so far gone in stupor that Gabriel's Horn itself is unlikely to have called him out of sleep.

Our first thought, nay, our only thought, was to raise anchor and head for open water, but we were denied even that chance. In less time than the blink of an eye a storm blew up, a wind so cold it would have frozen us to the deck if we hadn't had the foresight to wear our winter furs. Even at that, the cold bit at my nose so hard it felt like a nip from an excited dog.

"Up anchor," the First Mate shouted, but too late.

The sea had frozen solid around us.

We were stuck hard in place. Old timbers creaked and moaned as the ice gripped tight.

"Will she hold?" I asked the Mate.

"She held together when the ice was three feet thick off Newfoundland two years back," he said. "She'll hold now."

But I was starting to believe that it was colder yet than that day. I had to keep shifting from foot to foot; otherwise my soles would have frozen to the deck. By now snow fell so thick that I could no longer see the buildings of the colony beyond the dock.

"What purpose does it serve?" I said. I thought I had merely spoken to myself, but the Mate heard.

"The pastor used to say that everything, good or evil, was God's will, all part of a scheme of things, and that we would only ever understand when we were risen up on the Day of Judgment, and the veils would fall from our eyes."

"Then I wish the Day of Judgment would hurry upon us," I replied. "For I am sore perplexed, and have long since tired of this mummery."

"Be careful what you wish for, Cap'n," the Mate said. "Be very careful what you wish for."

Jim Crawford came up beside us on deck, musket in his hand. It fell unused to the deck when he saw what faced us across on the dock. Stout fellow though he was, Jim Crawford fell to his knees, struck down in terror.

"We're done for," he squealed.

The First Mate raised him to his feet.

"Not if we stand together as men," he said. "For truly that is the only way we will see home again. Cap'n... do I have your permission to break out the powder?"

"You have a plan?"

"More of an idea, but mayhap it will come to something."

"Then have at it man, have at it."

The Mate went below, while Crawford and I stood and watched the figures on the dockside.

They did not move. Their stares did not wander from where we stood. The snow got heavier yet, and still they did not stir.

"What do they want from us, Cap'n," Crawford wailed beside me. "What do they want?"

In truth, I could not answer him, for fear had taken hold deep within me. It would not be shifted, no matter how many prayers I uttered up to the most high. My eyes were fixed on the pastor and Bald Tom, two men as far apart in temperament as you are ever likely to meet. Yet here they were, standing side by side, joined in a new hatred against their former shipmates that I was at a loss to understand.

The wind howled. The snow bit into my cheeks, but I was loath to move, loath to take my eyes from the host on the dock lest they creep up on me unawares.

The First Mate came back onto deck, joined by Eye-

Tie Frank. They carried between them a half-barrel full of thick pitch.

"I've mixed in the powder," the First Mate said. "Remember yon corsair we met off the Azores?"

And indeed I did. In a flash I saw his plan.

"Will it burn against yon cold flesh?" I asked as I helped manhandle the barrel.

"I know nothing else that might," the Mate said.

He wrapped a linen cloth around the end of a broom-stick and dipped it in the pitch. He lit it from a small tinder box he kept in his waistcoat pocket.

"I trust no one but you with the flame," the Mate said, handing it to me.

I looked him in the eye, this man who had been my friend for past twenty years.

"It's risky," I said. "I have mind of what happened to Slant-Eyed Jock,"

"And I," the Mate said. "But I fear we have little choice."

He thrust his arm into the pitch. He came up with a handful of black ooze in his hand.

"Do it quick," he said. He thrust his hand towards me.

I lit the pitch. The Mate threw the lit mass away from him and it spluttered and spat as it sailed into the night. It hit Bald Tom on the chest, and ran down his torso, burning all the time.

The frozen man looked down, as if bemused. His whole face went up like a torch as the flame reached the powder that had been mixed in with the pitch.

Bald Tom fell to his knees, dropped forward. He tumbled off the dock and down to the frozen water below. He hit it hard, dropping through the ice with a sizzle and fountain of steam before he sank away out of sight, silent, like a stone.

Jim Crawford shouted in triumph, but the Mate hushed him sternly.

"I just killed a good man," he said grimly. "Tis no cause for celebration."

"He were dead already," Crawford said.

"That don't make me feel any better about it," the Mate said grimly.

He stuck his hand in the pitch again, and came up with a second ball.

"You were lucky with the first," I said. "Mayhap it is best not to chance it again?"

"We both know we have no other choice, Cap'n. Light it up."

For a second time his arm seemed to grow a flame. The powder in the pitch spluttered before it left his hand. He threw it towards the dock, but it exploded and fizzled out well short, dropping away out of sight to the ice below.

"I can do better than that," Crawford said.

Before either of us could stop him he plunged his whole arm into the pitch, coming up with a far bigger ball than the Mate. He leaned forward and touched the flame to the oily mixture.

His arm immediately burst aflame, fire roaring up the side of his head, flesh crisping and melting. He screamed, just once, and fell away from us. The powder went up and the whole right hand side of Crawford's body burst, like a ripe fruit, a dead, smoking ruin before he hit the deck.

The Mate looked down at what was left of the man. "Be careful," I said.

The Mate bent to get himself another handful, when Eye-Tie Frank stepped in front of him.

"Mayhap I have a better method," he said. He removed his cap, then his belt. He filled his cap with the pitch, and then tied it up with his belt. He was left with a two foot length of belt with a ball of pitch on the end.

"Shame on you," he said to the Mate and me, his slight accent showing through. "Do you not do this yourselves at home to bring in the New Year?"

He lit the pitch, swung it around his head and sent in winging over the dock.

"That we do," the Mate said, unbuckling his own belt. "Although I am usually too far gone in my cups to remember it."

The fireball exploded just above the heads of the throng of the dead, sending burning flame over five of them.

The Mate sent one of his own after it. The air filled with black acrid smoke as flesh burned. The ranks of the dead did not move, even as their neighbours burned.

"All very well," the Mate said. "But we have a limited supply of belts and caps. And I'd rather my breeches didn't fall down... not in this weather."

Dave the Bosun's mate arrived on deck. We set him to finding twine and cloth, the better to make more fireballs.

For a while the air was full of flame and fury.

The snow got heavier still. Sometimes we could not even see the dock, but the smell of burning meat told us we still hit our targets.

We lost ourselves in a world of burning pitch and whirling snow, the only sound being the coughing, spluttering rattle of powder starting to fizzle, and the whoosh of flame as we hit our targets. The night went on without end.

I know not when the snow finally stopped, only that I looked up to see stars and a full moon overhead.

"My eyes deceive me, Cap'n," the Mate said beside me. "For surely the moon was on the wane when we hove-to here."

"There is deception here, right enough," I replied, "But it is not your eyes. It comes from that one."

Out over the dockside, the white native with the feather chest still stood tall and un-burnt. Around him the ranks of the dead lay, finally at rest, a smoking chaos of limbs and torsos piled higgeldy-piggeldly in a hellish landscape strewn across the dock.

The native thumped at his chest. He made an expansive circle with his arms before thumping his chest again.

He did this twice before I realized his meaning.

This land is mine.

He pointed at Dave the Bosun's mate. The man jerked, as if jolted by lightning.

To our astonishment he threw himself off the boat, towards the pier.

It was a prodigious leap. I would not have placed a bet on him achieving it, but he seemed to have been given wings. He landed, a few feet in front of the white native.

The native thumped his chest again. He stroked Dave's face, gently, as if romancing a woman. Once more we had to watch a colleague freeze. His body went stiff, and a last plume of breath left him, floating high in the air. I could only hope it was his soul, fleeing to its place in Paradise, for the thought of a man being frozen but yet imprisoned, mute, in his own body, was almost too much to bear.

Finally Dave turned back towards us, blind white eyes staring out of a blue face. The native once more made the circle with his arms.

"He's showing us," the Mate said. "He's showing us that all this is his... including us."

"It does not include me," Eye-Tie Frank said. He leapt off the ship, screaming his defiance. Whether he intended to reach the pier itself we shall never know. His leap was well short and he fell away below our sight, never to be heard of again.

The native stared at the two of us, his black-lipped mouth raised in a smile. He thumped his chest again. Somewhere, out in the wild reaches of the night, a wolf howled at the moon. It was answered, much closer, by a pack, a wild, ululating wail that seemed to pierce my very skull.

The First Mate looked at me, and I at him.

"We have served together over twenty years, Cap'n. I have been proud to call you my friend."

"And I you," I replied. We both had a tear in our eye, there at the end.

"Goodbye, Cap'n," he said, as the native on the dock pointed a long white finger, straight at him.

What happened next will stay with me for the remainder of what is left of my life.

The First Mate shook and juddered, in the same

manner as Dave the Bosun's mate had done a few moments before. He gritted his teeth. He stuck both arms into the pitch, all the way up to his shoulders. Before I could move, he took the torch from me. He leapt from the boat, straight at the native.

"Havenhome!" he called, his voice ringing out loud and clear in the night. He landed just in front of the tall white figure, stepped forward, and grabbed it in a tight embrace. I have seen men's backs broken by that grip, but the native ne'er flinched. The Mate put all his strength into it, but the white figure was unbowed.

Then, at the last, as the skin in the Mate's face went blue, he yelled out once more, a formless word. He brought down the torch, and set light to his pitch covered arms.

I stood and watched, with tears running through a grim smile, as the pair of them burned. The feather crown went first, blazing all as one and sending flames up the creature's back. Where the First Mate's pitch-covered arms touched its body they stuck, searing huge patches of flesh at a time.

Together the bodies fell on the dock. The Mate was surely dead by now, but the creature could not escape from his embrace.

Even then I thought the creature might break free, for the flames had begun to die down, yet clearly, it still showed sign of what passed for life in that white frozen frame.

Finally, just as I was starting to despair, the powder in the pitch took.

A yellow flame shot ten yards into the sky. When it died down there was nothing left of either body that could be recognized... just one single, fused mass of blackened flesh.

~-o0O0o-~

I am decided. This will be my last ever entry in this journal, made in the hope that what is related may help some other Christian souls from sharing the fate of my crewmates. In the meantime I can do little more than offer up prayers, for the First Mate, and all the other brave men of the Havenhome who will ne'er return home.

This proud ship, my home these many years, has sailed its last, and I am no longer Captain of anything other than my own soul. In truth, I do not think I will ever be able to lead men again. If I make it to home port alive I will retire.

I will spend my time supping beer in the harbour and telling tall tales with the other old gentleman, content to keep my feet warm before the fires of hearth and home.

But that seems like a long way off, another lifetime where the sun shines hot and yellow on the fields, and my Lizzie stands at the door, smiling. I have some of the Havenhome's tale yet to tell before I can begin my journey towards that most welcome of sights.

After the Mate had made his sacrifice I could do naught but stand there, staring at the smoking ruin of all that was left of my friends and shipmates. I paid particular attention to the charred mass where lay the Mate and the native, half expecting at any moment that a white figure would rise from the dockside to mock me once more.

Nothing moved except the stirring of acrid smoke on the breeze.

The wind died, like the last sigh of an old man on his death-bed. A cloud ran over the full moon. Slowly at first, then faster until water ran in runnels off the deck; the snow thawed.

And still I stood there, long into the night, long after the sun came up and the last of the frost was taken by the morning.

I felt empty, devoid of action, abandoned by hope. I was only brought out of my reverie by old Stumpy Jack, who emerged, blinking into the sunlight, looking near as dead as some of those lying on the dockside.

"Are we alive, Cap'n?" he said, "or in Paradise?"

"Does this look like any Paradise you might expect?" I said.

He stood beside me for a long time, staring out over the smoking dock.

"Is it over?" he whispered.

"I know not whether it will ever be over," I replied. "But it is over for now."

It was Stumpy Jack who brought me inside, him who made me drink and eat, that I might stay alive when all of my brethren lay dead around us.

And even now, while I write this, the old man is showing more fortitude than I thought he possessed. He has brought the remains of the Mate and the native inside the ship.

"The rest of them, Cap'n? What shall we do with the rest of them?"

There are bodies, mostly charred and unrecognizable, strewn all across the dock. The Mate's pitch and powder concoction did for them all in the end.

"By rights, these people deserve a Christian burial," I said.

"Nay, Cap'n," Old Stumpy said. "Whatever part of them belonged to the Lord has already gone. And neither you nor I have the strength, or the heart, to waste in spending another night near this place."

I reluctantly had to agree with him.

We will scuttle the Havenhome here, on this dock. I will leave my journal in my chest, wrapped in oilskins. In that manner, if anyone should chance on the drowned boat, they may, if the Lord is with them, find this journal first, and stop before they unleash what Jack and I have left at the bottom of the hold.

We have gathered our provisions. We will leave tonight. The only other thing I take with me from my cabin is my bible, in the hope it will give me solace in the nights to come. But I fear I will ne'er find hope again in the words of the Lord, for I know the pastor's white eyes will ever accuse me, even in the deepest depths of slumber. If the Lord did not see fit to save such a holy and devout man as the pastor, what hope is there for the likes of me, who has done so many things that require repentance?

Forgive me Lizzie, for I know now you will never read this. But if the Lord gives me strength, I intend to head down the coast, for warmer climes and friendly company. Mayhap I shall return yet to home port, and your soft arms.

You will fill my dreams until I am once more at your side. Be well, my love. Be well for both of us.

Your loving husband, John.

The Yule Log

John took the best part of a week in choosing the right tree and another day deciding which branch would be sacrificed. After a further day he had the sawn-off log cleared of particularly resistant lichen that had taken hold in the crook of a branch. Only then was he ready. He clamped the log tight to his workbench, made sure the chisel was sharp, and began.

He cried as he carved; the memory of her singing always brought tears, her pure soprano climbing above his ponderous chord changes on the wheezing harmonium.

Jacqueline.

It took a longish time to get her name engraved in the log. The cold didn't help, biting deep into old bones despite the furnace in the corner of the workshop. After the name was done he had to work fast, for it was already dusk and the log needed to be in the grate before midnight, otherwise it would all have been for naught.

He quickly chiselled out the second line; words long since etched on his memory.

Ae fond kiss.

He carried the log through to the main cottage and took care preparing a fire, using just the right mixture of paper and coal to ensure that the log would not burn too quickly when placed in the front of the grate. That done he went to the dresser and carefully retrieved a charred piece of wood from where it had been wrapped in a handkerchief. He thrust it deep into the bowels of the coal and lit the dry paper with a match.

Once he was satisfied the fire wouldn't go out, he prepared the next part of the ritual – three fingers of single malt in a glass by his chair, and enough tobacco to see him through the night. The log cracked and spat as he filled his first pipe. Almost immediately he was lost in reverie.

It will take time.

She has gone to a better place.

For most of the year he managed to believe, helped by mindless toil in the fields, hard liquor at night, and the crumbs of comfort that came from faith. But on this, the anniversary of the day she was taken from him, faith proved harder to come by. Everywhere he looked he saw her traces; from the mirror above the mantel they'd got as a wedding present from her father to the walnut pipe in his hand that the same old man had smoked all his adult life.

John did not notice the tears that ran down his cheeks until he was brought back to the present by the church bells calling the faithful to midnight mass.

There was a time when he would have walked the snowy lane to the church, arm in arm with Jackie, stars twinkling in her eyes. Those walks had stopped all too suddenly, the end coming as they got ready for Mass that fateful night. First came a headache, then a fit, and then she was gone. A doctor, a policeman and the vicar, three wise men, ushered her off to the great beyond.

Now John sat, with the log burning, waiting for a sign that another year was worth the effort. Carols whispered in the night across the cold air between his cottage and the church. Snow pattered on the window in an accompanying beat. Fresh tears came, and suddenly John was weeping uncontrollably. The old harmonium in the corner moaned in sympathy.

He looked up from the fire to where a quick movement in the mirror caught his eye.

Jackie?

Cold lips brushed at his cheek, tears freezing in his whiskers.

A high, soprano voice carried through the room, just audible above the moan of the instrument.

Ae fond kiss.

John sat upright in his chair, and in the process knocked the whisky glass over. It clattered on the floorboards. The harmonium stilled. Outside the snow died to a mere rustle. Over at the church the congregation was between carols. Silence fell.

Did I imagine it?

The next thought came immediately.

Does it matter?

He sat in the chair all night. In the morning he took a charred portion of the log from the cooling grate. He wrapped it in a handkerchief and put it away in the dresser. He felt refreshed. As he closed the drawer he sang the words that would see him through another year.

Ae fond kiss.
And then we sever.

Living the Dream

In the dream the house looks older, more dilapidated. A crack runs from the lintel of the front door all the way to the guttering, and the climbing rose – the one outstanding feature – has withered and died, its dry stems crawling like wrinkles across the walls.

The Watcher stands on the doorstep, listening, waiting for the noise that always comes. Autumn leaves flutter around in the sudden breeze, but still the Watcher cannot move.

The front door rattles, as if someone is vainly trying to get out. The Watcher's eyes are drawn to the gap underneath it – remembering how the wind whistles through, bringing its chill to the whole house. The door rattles again, but that still isn't it.

And then it comes, the soft thud, as of a chopper on bone.

A red flood gushes from under the door – a roaring wave of blood that washes the Watcher away and down into a blackness from which there is no return.

~-o0O0o-~

John Thorne sat upright in bed, breath coming in hot gasps.

What the hell was that all about?

The shadows in his room had no answers for him. He lay awake for almost an hour as the moonlight crawled across the ceiling, but sleep stayed away. In the end he got out of bed and went to the kitchen. While he was making a sandwich the dream stayed fresh in his mind. He felt strange, almost guilty, as if he'd been caught masturbating.

And where did all that blood come from?

Thorne wasn't a deep thinker, and his imagination did not stretch as far as positing any supernatural agency, but it had felt almost as if someone else had been inside his head.

Too much cheese before bed makes for a restless night.

He could almost *hear* his old mum say it – *she* would always be inside his head.

The acts of domesticity involved in putting together the bread, butter and sardines rooted him back in reality and finally the dream faded, leaving just a memory... of wind and blood.

He munched on the sandwich as he headed back upstairs and dropped back into bed. By twenty past three he was fast asleep. In the morning the dream had faded to little more than a memory of a disturbed night. When he left the house after breakfast he felt a breeze at his heels and something stirred in his mind, but that too was forgotten as work blew everything else away in a flurry of crates to be stacked and floors to be swept.

That all changed late afternoon. He had just the main loading bay of the factory left to sweep. Mary Carruthers, the administrator, came out of her office, red-faced and puffing. It was a hot day and she carried at least a hundred pounds more than she aught to. On days like this, every one of those pounds showed. Normally Thorne wouldn't have given her another look but she chose that moment to drop a pen and, with her back to him, bent to pick it up.

Her skirt rode up the back of her legs above the knee and Thorne got a clear look all the way up to where the thick white maggots of her thighs tried to squeeze themselves into a crevasse protected by a pair of pink panties. He was suddenly embarrassed by an erection, and he pretended to sweep the floor harder while hunching over to avoid it being spotted.

"Are you OK?" the Carruthers woman asked. She had come across the factory floor and was only feet away. Thorne mumbled something in reply, desperately hoping she would not look down. But she kept her gaze on his face, and she even looked concerned. Thorne's embarrassment grew and he felt heat at his cheeks.

"Mr. Thorne?" She reached out a hand towards him. Instinctively he shuffled away. He saw the hurt look that passed across the administrator's face.

"Sorry," he mumbled, looking at his feet, but when he looked up she was walking away towards the car park beyond the loading bay doors.

The erection stayed for a while longer.

He kept sweeping for a while, hoping that the tumescence would recede, but the image kept returning, the expanse of thighs, and the merest *hint* of pink between them.

If this keeps up I'm going to have to tape it down.

But it did keep up, and Thorne cut a peculiar shuffling figure as he made his way home.

Later, once he was settled in front of the TV, he found the image of those thighs overlaying everything he watched until he had to switch off the TV and sit, in the dark, staring at the small patch of pink. He felt hot, prickly, ants crawling just under his skin. A shower only made things worse, leaving him all too aware of his pink nakedness. Disgusted with himself he left the house.

A cool breeze blew around his ankles as he closed the door behind him.

~-o0O0o-~

At first he was content to walk aimlessly, letting his mind wander. It only wanted to wander in one direction. Without consciously thinking, he arrived outside the Carruthers woman's house. It was near dark, but she hadn't yet drawn the curtains. Thorne crept closer, using the mature shrubbery in her garden as cover. As soon as he saw the woman sitting on a couch in front of the TV his erection swelled. He caressed it gently as he watched. The woman crossed her legs, and a sudden burst of heat washed through Thorne, as if a firecracker had gone off inside his head.

Someone shouted.

"Hey! What are you doing there?"

Thorne ran, feet banging hard on the sidewalk. More shouts echoed behind him but he scarcely heard. It was only when he got home he realized that his cheeks hurt.

He had smiled all the way back.

The next day he made a point of sweeping outside her office more often than usual. She never looked up from the pile of papers on her desk but that was OK with Thorne – it allowed him to watch... watch and dream. From where he stood he could see the side of her thigh as it pressed up tight against the material of her thin business skirt. He felt the erection swell and moved away to the far end of the factory before it could embarrass him again.

He had to limit himself. There were people around on the factory floor who might notice that he was spending *too* much time in one place. He contented himself with small glimpses of her, but each one brought the *need* closer to the fore.

The dreams got more intense after that.

~-o0Oo-~

The Watcher is in the bedroom, standing in the corner. A woman cowers on the bed, the quilt tucked tight under her chin. The Watcher wants to tell the woman that everything will be all right.

But that would be a lie.

A half eaten sandwich sits on the bedside table, but the woman does not even look at it – her eyes are focused on the door, waiting. The television is still on downstairs, but the Watcher knows that the woman is not safe, that she will never be safe.

The Watcher sees the woman's eyes open wider as the sound of footsteps echo in the stairwell. The man comes in. He is naked. His eyes are black pools of shadow as he moves to the side of the bed and pulls aside the quilt.

The woman's body is thin, painfully so, each of her ribs showing a proud ridge in her flesh. She used to be heftier, a hundred pounds that were a hundred too many on hot Summer's days. Her skin is china white, almost translucent and that only serves to accentuate the bruises.

He hits her, twice, once on each cheek and her head jerks like a marionette, first right then left. She falls back in the bed, her legs pushed tightly together, and even tighter still when he tries to prise them apart. He hits her in the stomach, just one punch, but it causes her to curl up in a ball. Her buttocks point at him, and that is all the excuse he needs. He moves forward, lips wet with anticipation.

~-o0O0o-~

Thorne came awake with a start, eyes wild and chest heaving. His hand went to his groin and came away damp.

You sick bastard.

He stayed there playing with his limp penis and reliving the dream until he was hard. Then he made it nice again. With his come still drying on his belly he wandered through the house, singing to himself – nonsense mouth music. As he moved through the rooms he masturbated, leaving spatters on the carpets – marking his territory.

That was just the start of many wet nights, every dream involving him inflicting atrocities on the body of an increasingly weak office administrator.

He spent his evenings in the bushes outside her house. At first he was nervous, waiting for another shout, another discovery. But as nights went by and he was not challenged, he got bolder. Eventually he was able to press up so close that he had a nose against the window. After dark, when she closed the curtains, they hung slightly apart, giving him a half-inch window into her life. He had an uninterrupted view of her couch as she watched TV and he watched her. She had a way of hitching up her skirt to get comfortable that kept him there for hours.

At work he found it hard to keep away from her. He made excuses to be outside her office, just to catch a glimpse of ankle, the flash of a bra through a gape in her blouse. That sustained him until the next evening.

He kept notes on her activities, looking for patterns so he might be more able to predict when the *good* nights would be – the ones where she sat on the sofa in her nightgown, legs slightly open, as if inviting him to step through the glass and join her.

He thought he was being discreet, especially at work. But one day, as he was approaching her office door, he found her standing there, watching him.

"Can I have a word, Mr. Thorne?" she said, and motioned him into the office, closing the door behind them. She directed him to the chair opposite hers and sat down at her desk. He couldn't see her legs, but he imagined the skirt riding up at her thighs, and had to cross his own legs quickly to hide his ardour.

"Mr. Thorne?" she said. He looked up. She was staring straight at him, a small smile on her lips. He looked away quickly. He had no interest in her face. Instead he stared at a point over her left shoulder, not trusting himself to look anywhere else.

Her next words sent a jolt through him that almost knocked him off his chair.

"I've been watching you, Mr. Thorne."
She knows!

"It's OK," she said softly, and with more than a hint of sorrow. "I know all about crushes. I just wanted to nip this one in the bud before it goes any further. We can't have you hanging around my office. People will talk."

He *wanted* to say something, but words wouldn't come. He looked at her, but the sad smile on her face wasn't anything he wanted to see and he went back to staring over her shoulder.

"We all have our dreams, Mr. Thorne," she said. "But that's all it can be – a dream. You do see that don't you?"

He nodded, grunted, and suddenly the chat was over and he was shown the door.

But I have learned something.
She's a dreamer.
She's just like me.

~-oOOo-~

Thorne spent his evenings at her window, and his nights in feverish dreams that came out of nowhere and sent him into paroxysms of wanking frenzy.

He came to know her patterns, how he had to get to the window early on Tuesday and Friday as she settled down to watch a soap opera on the TV. And on Saturdays she treated herself – wine and chocolate and a movie with swelling chords that always made her cry.

That didn't bother him.

It's not her face I'm interested in.

And that might have been that, each of them living their dreams.

Until the day she pissed him off.

He arrived outside her window just as night was falling. Summer was almost over, and the nights were getting longer. He looked forward to Fall and Winter with mounting anticipation, imagining all the extra hours of *fun*. But there was no fun to be had. When he pressed his nose to the glass all he could see was the TV and one corner of the sofa.

She's rearranged the furniture!

He almost screamed. He watched as she came into the room... then walked out of view.

He banged a fist against the window. Before he could move she pulled the curtains open... and looked straight at him. He ran – surprised as he left her garden that there were no screams following him. Once at home he lay awake for hours, waiting for a knock on the door, for the police to begin his humiliation. But no one came.

He dragged himself out of bed when the alarm went off and ran a hot bath. He relived one moment over and over, trying to picture her face as she threw open the curtains. Was that surprise he saw there? Or was it something else?

Something like acceptance?

She didn't scream. Maybe she has always known I was there? Has she been performing all this time? Performing just for me?

The dreams also kept replaying in his mind, each as vivid as the other, and as he lay in the steaming bath he wasn't surprised to find his erection growing again. He lay back and closed his eyes – waiting.

There was more to see.

~-o0O0o-~

The Watcher is standing at the bathroom door as the woman is bathed.

The man has her held under the cold tap, but she does not struggle. Her limbs barely move and he has to lift her arms to get at the fine down of hair in the armpits. He scrubs her, hard, with a coarse brush – its tough bristles turning her skin to a tracery of red, sores and welts blossoming among the yellow-black bruises as the soap suds run pinkly down the white porcelain.

He lays her down in the bath and stands for long seconds looking down at her. He takes in the thin bruised body and his lips purse in disappointment. But it is the look in her eyes that sends him over the edge – there is no spark left – no fight.

This one is all used up.

He lifts an open razor from the sink and climbs into the bath with her, his folds of fat rippling in anticipation.

As his weight settles on top of the woman she lets out a sigh – more an exhaled breath than an intimation of pain, but it is enough to get him started.

He makes the first cut just above the navel.

~-o0O0o-~

Thorne woke still sitting in a tub of rapidly cooling water, knowing what had to be done.

He made it across town just in time. The woman came out of her front door and looked carefully around before venturing from the porch. It didn't help her any.

Thorne had a hand at her throat and a knife at her neck before she had gone two steps.

"One word, and I'll cut you," he whispered.

She nodded, eyes already red and puffy with fresh tears as he led her to his car.

He made her lie behind the driver's seat all the way.

"Please, Mr. Thorne," she said softly. "This isn't necessary you know. We could be friends."

He showed her the knife. She went quiet. Her eyes continued to plead with him, but the dreams had shown him what was coming. He couldn't deny them.

He was hard again as he dragged her into his house. This early in the morning there was no one around to see him, but he wasn't even sure he cared. All he wanted to do was get her inside to where he could get started.

She didn't protest as he pushed her up the stairs, but more tears rolled down her cheeks. Her make-up ran, and she smudged it all across her face, giving her the look of a manic clown.

That's not right. That's just not right.

He threw her into the bath and held her under the cold tap as he undressed her. She did not struggle. Her limbs barely moved and he had to lift her arms to get at the fine down of hair in the armpits. He scrubbed her, hard, with a coarse brush, its tough bristles turning her skin to a tracery of red, welts blossoming as the soap suds ran pinkly down the white porcelain.

He laid her down in the bath and stood for long seconds looking down at her.

What's wrong with this picture?

It took him several seconds to come to the

realization. This wasn't like the dream. Something was wrong... something vital.

She's too fat.

His erection went limp as quickly as it had come. He dragged her roughly from the bath and threw her on the bed in the spare room, tying her down with an old clothes line, tightly enough to raise fresh welts at her ankles and wrists. That brought fresh stirring at his groin, but nothing that needed any fixing.

Not yet.

"Please," she whispered.

He wasn't about to allow any more of *that*. He taped her mouth with duct-tape and went downstairs. He sat in his armchair and listened. There was no sound from above.

It's as if she's not even really here.

He went to work and managed to act concerned when Mrs. Carruthers failed to show up at her office. People came and went during the day, and at one point the police arrived, but Thorne kept his head down. No one paid him any attention at all.

When he got home the house felt different, somehow *fuller*. As he walked through the front door a cool breeze played at his ankles, a portent of winter to come.

And long dark nights of fun.

He was almost surprised to find her there on the bed in the spare room. She'd been crying again, and moaned quietly at him through the duct tape. Goose-pimples sowed along the full length of her body so he laid an old quilt on her.

I'm not a cruel man.

During that first evening he checked on her often,

but over the coming days – days that stretched into weeks – his visits to the upstairs room grew less frequent.

He lived for the dreams.

~-o0Oo-~

The Watcher is in the bedroom – just standing in the corner. A woman cowers on the bed, the quilt tucked tight under her chin. The Watcher wants to tell the woman that everything will be all right.

But that would be a lie.

~-o0Oo-~

He woke, sitting upright in the armchair. The TV showed only white static, messages from the beginning of time. Something *creaked* above him, like a body weight shifting.

The Watcher!

He was up and heading for the stairs before he realized the stupidity of his action.

You're the Watcher you idiot.

But he still checked the corner of the room when he got there... just to be sure. A breeze cooled his ankles, and shadows moved in a swirl, but he paid them little heed. The woman cowered on the bed.

He pulled aside the quilt. The woman's body thin, painfully so, each of her ribs showing a proud ridge in her flesh. Her skin looked almost translucent.

It's time.

He undid the ties, tearing off strips of pink-tinged

flesh along with the line in his eagerness to get started.

The woman still had some fight in her. She swiped a hand at his face, fingernails grown torn and ragged raising a trio of welts on his face. He slapped her, twice, once on each cheek and her head jerked like a marionette, first right then left. She fell back in the bed, her legs pushed tightly together. He hit her in the stomach, just one punch, but it caused her to curl up in a ball. Her buttocks pointed at him, and that was all the excuse he needed.

He moved forward, lips wet with anticipation.

Once he was done she had no fight left in her, but he tied her up again, just in case. As he left the room a cool breeze played around his lower legs, and a black shadow shifted in the corner, but Thorne was too *full* to pay any notice. He had a broad smile on his face as he went back downstairs.

I'm living the dream.

That night the Watcher was there again.

~-o0O0o-~

The Watcher stands at the door of the house, listening. And then it comes, the soft thud, as of a chopper on bone.

The Watcher moves forward and pushes the door open.

Inside everything is red. The Watcher heads for the stairs. A wind howls through the house like a scream, the walls pulsing in time with a frightened heartbeat. The noise seems to be coming from the bedroom at the top of the stairs. The Watcher heads in that direction and walks inside.

The room is empty, just a bundle of bloody rags on the bed.

~-oOOo-~

Thorne woke once more sitting in the downstairs armchair.

That's not right. Something's changed. That's not how the dream goes.

He made for the stairs. He stopped just before going into the bedroom.

What do I do if she isn't there?

But that wasn't an option. He was living the dream, and the dream waited for him, just beyond the door.

He went inside.

The woman lay there, staring straight at the ceiling, not even seeing him.

"I'm living the dream," he whispered.

He undid her bonds and carried her to the bathroom, laying her down in the bath and standing for long seconds looking down at her. He took in the thin bruised body and his lips pursed in disappointment. But it was the look in her eyes that sent him over the edge – there was no spark left, no fight.

She's all used up.

He lifted an open razor from the sink and climbed into the bath with her, his folds of fat rippling in anticipation. A cool breeze came from beyond the door, raising the hairs at the back of his thighs, but by now he was too busy to notice.

As his weight settled on top of the woman she let out

a sigh – more an exhaled breath than an intimation of pain, but it was enough to get him started.

He made his first cut just above the navel.

There were no screams, no exhortations – only a painful acceptance and, deep down, a longing for release.

In the corner of the room behind him dark shadows gathered.

His cuts got more frenzied as he searched for deeper pleasures. With one thrust of the razor he opened her from groin to chest, and this time he was rewarded with a moan – a small thing, but a sign of possibilities. He gloated over the small intestines as they glistened, marvelling at their hot life before reaching into the gore and, both hands already red, began to pull. She screamed one last time as her guts reeled from her body and Thorne rolled around in them, revelling in the heat and the stink. His penis jerked, once, twice, in spasm as he spurted long and hard into the body cavity.

He lay there on top of the husk that was all that remained of the woman, lost in an ecstasy that threatened to engulf him completely.

The body was cold and sticky by the time he prised himself out of the tub. A breeze blew, bringing a snell winter to the bathroom and an icy touch to the tiles underfoot. A dark shadow loomed in the corner, catching Thorne's eye. He turned in that direction.

I've been watching you, Mr. Thorne, a cold voice whispered.

Mrs. Carruthers stood there, a heavy meat cleaver in her hand. She wore her black, no nonsense, business suit, the skirt hitched up to show smooth white thighs and the merest glimpse of pink panties.

She's put the weight back on.

She came out of the corner slowly, gliding, as if on smooth, soundless wheels. Thorne backed away, whimpering, until he felt the cold tub behind his knees.

Living the dream, the Watcher whispered, raising the cleaver.

Thorne fell back into the tub, his last scream cut short.

And then it comes, the soft thud, as of a chopper on bone.

The Shoogling Jenny

I found the lyric I sought in a small town in the Appalachians. I'd been looking for the origins of the song for some time, but now I wish I had never heard it. It is a hard story to tell, but I'm setting it down here and leaving it in the archive in the hope that it might dissuade others from following in my footsteps.

It started in hope. Even the long drive after an even longer flight failed to dampen my enthusiasm. I was on the trail of something that would justify the money the Miner's Union had given me – I would prove a link between Scottish and Appalachian mining songs.

And I might even find the one song that unites the traditions.

That was the golden ring, and I felt nearer to it than ever. The nights spent poring over dusty books in badly lit rooms were about to pay off. After checking in to my hotel I wasted no time in getting down to business. I asked to be directed to the miner's bar.

Every mining town has one – the place where the men go to wind down and gripe about conditions. I found that in this regard Appalachia was no different to Scotland – on entering the bar I immediately felt at home. Country-blues played in the background, and was punctuated by the clack and thud from the pool table. The murmur of conversation was a low constant hum that only stilled briefly as I entered. Even the faces looked familiar – ingrained grime and a paleness won by years spent in the dark, tired eyes deep set under heavy brows.

I had grown up in places like this, and even the local accent held a twang that wouldn't be out of place in a Scottish community. I bought a beer and sat, taking in the atmosphere before getting down to business.

The barman immediately knew the person I needed to speak to.

"Jack Green's your man," he said. "Over there in the corner. He knows the history of the mine better than anyone else."

Jack proved more taciturn than I'd have liked, but a brace of beers loosened him up somewhat. We talked for some time about mining songs in general, and I told him of my quest to find links across the ocean. He seemed genuinely interested as I told him of my viewing in Cambridge of the original manuscripts of Sharp and Karpeles' tour, and of the note in handwriting on the page, the scrawl that had brought me all the way to this bar.

"The tale of the Shoogling Jenny has been removed at the request of the mine owner."

Those words had been like a light going on over my head, for I well knew the song, having heard it from my own grandfather many years before. If I could show it came from this mine, it would make a fine central linking motif for my book.

I sang the first few lines for him, softly so that only he would hear.

Tam was a miner born and bred, he worked hard for his penny
Tam had a love and she turned his head, and her name was Shoogling Jenny

I hadn't noticed Jack Green had gone quiet.

"I know the song you mean," he said softly. "We call it *Shaking Jinny*. But I wouldn't go around this town asking questions about it. It ain't been sung in these parts for fifty years and more."

"Why?"

He refused to say. Even four more beers wouldn't sway him. All I got out of him was a name.

"Tom Malone," he said as I stood to leave. "The mine owner. If anybody will talk to you, it's Malone. But I didn't tell you that."

I took my leave and made a call, setting up a meeting with Malone in the morning. I told him I was researching links to the Scottish mining community, and he seemed happy to talk to me. Then again, I didn't mention the song. Maybe if I had things might have gone differently.

I stayed in the bar too long that night – I guess I felt *too* at home. The beer flowed freely, and the locals were only too happy to share anecdotes about the mine and its history. I remained just sober enough to remember Jack Green's warning about the *Shoogling Jenny* and I kept quiet on the subject, hoping that the next day would yield the long hoped for result.

It was late by the time I dragged myself to bed. They had left the heating on too high and the room felt stifling, threatening to send my already unsteady head swirling. I turned it down and threw the window open. At first all I noticed was the pounding of blood in my ears, then I heard, from a great distance, a well-known refrain.

167

*The rails they ran both fast and true, as fast and true
as any*
*And for all I know she runs there still, the birling,
Shoogling, Jenny.*

And as quickly as that I felt too cold and far too
sober. A shiver ran through me, forcing me to retreat to
the too-warm room. I raided the mini-bar for some
Scotch and watched a glossy cop show on cable with
unseeing eyes. I still heard the song in my head, and it
was there when I lay down fully clothed, and fell into a
restless sleep.

In the morning the hangover was the foremost thing
in my mind, but even as I showered the tune still ran,
and I had to stop from bursting into an impromptu
rendition. I tried to focus on basics – coffee, breakfast
and the making of notes prior to my meeting with
Malone. I felt almost human by the time I walked
through town to the mine's main office building.

Tom Malone proved to be younger than expected –
fresh faced in a smart suit with a smile that was just a
fraction short of sincere. Over more coffee we talked
about the purpose of my trip and the *Shoogling Jenny* in
particular. Unlike the miners in the bar, he seemed more
than happy to expound at length on the song.

Indeed, his very first statement almost floored me.

"It's a true story you know?" he said. Before I could
reply he burst into song, a fine high baritone that rang
through the room.

*Now the boss Malone was a jealous man, and Jenny
was his lass*

So he followed Tam down to the hole, and shot him in the back.

He stopped and looked straight at me.

"Malone... my great-great-grandfather. I've been hearing the story since I was a lad – how Tam seduced his woman, and how Great-Great-Granddaddy killed Tam and stuck him in a cart."

"The original '*Shoogling Jenny*?'"

Malone smiled. "That's right," he said, waving his hands theatrically. "The haunted mine cart – the excuse of miners everywhere for not doing any work. Old wives tales... I'm sure you've got *plenty* of them where you come from."

I managed a smile in return. "Several. But none with any truth to them," I said. "What I need for my book is physical verification – an old transcript of the song maybe?"

Malone laughed. "I don't know about transcripts," he said. "But if it's physical verification you want, you've come to the right place. Tell me... have you ever actually been down a mineshaft?"

Five minutes later we were in a metal cab heading down into the darkness. He had changed the suit for a set of orange overalls, but he still looked too clean, too neat for this place. Three miners shared the trip down with us, but none of them looked at Malone or even acknowledged his presence during the ten-minute descent.

We arrived in a well-lit tunnel that hummed with the sound of a conveyer belt taking fresh-dug coal to a series of carts that were hauled in a continuous stream back up the shaft. That wasn't what he'd brought me to see though. We walked down an older shaft for maybe five minutes.

"This is where it happened," he said. "Great-Great-Granddaddy found Tam and Jenny down here. They thought they were safe... but the old man knew better."

He led me up a slight incline to a chamber, dimly lit with only a single flickering light bulb. Two old carts sat there, the nearest half-on, half-off the old rails.

"You wanted *physical verification*?" he said. "Here you go." He patted the nearest cart. "Meet the one, the only, the original... *Shoogling Jenny.*"

He raised his voice and sang again.

Now Jenny wouldn't leave her man, and clung to him real hard
Malone in his rage shot her too, and left them in the dark.

He rapped his hand on the cart.

"Come out come out wherever you are."

Suddenly everything went quiet. I couldn't hear any sound from the other shafts of the mine. The light bulb flickered overhead.

"Come on over," Malone said, still standing over the cart. "This is what you came for isn't it? The old man dumped the bodies here. From what I heard Tam took his time dying."

And Tam he drew his dying breath, and cursed baith lang and sare
And though Malone might own the mine, he was

happy never mare.

I backed away. The cold chill was back, the same as I'd felt at the window the night before, and suddenly all I wanted was another beer. Malone seemed not to notice. He slapped the cart again. It shook on the rail, rattling once then went quiet.

They say at night when the moon is full, that Shoogling Jenny runs there still.

"What do you think?" Malone said. "Is it a full moon?"

His laugh sounded cold and cruel.

I backed off further. "I'd like to go now," I said.

He smiled, his teeth showing white in the dim light. He walked towards me.

"I took you for a rational man," he said as he walked back down to me.

I wasn't watching him. My gaze was fixed on the cart at the top of the slope. It rocked from side to side on the rusted rail, as if keeping a beat.

Malone stood halfway down the slope.

"Come on, man. You're not afraid of the dark are you? I thought you Scots were a practical bunch. You surely don't believe that old song? *And though Malone might own the mine, he was happy never mare?* I've never been happier."

The cart rocked hard, settled on the rail, and rolled, gaining speed as it came down the incline. I couldn't take my eyes off the front wheel – the one that shook and *shoogled* all the way down.

"Look out," I shouted, but that only made him turn to see what was going on. It hit him at waist height, knocking him out of his shoes and sending him sprawling on the track. The sound as his neck broke was the loudest thing I heard that day.

But that wasn't the worst of it. The thing that still sends me screaming out of sleep at nights was the last thing I saw before a faint took me.

The cart rolled – *up the incline* – then came back down hard to finish the job. And just as darkness took me, I heard the singing again, two voices, a man and a woman, high and ethereal in the distance, joined forever in song.

The rails they run both fast and true, as fast and true as any

And for all I know she runs there still, the birling, Shoogling, Jenny.

The Haunting of Esther Cox

Extract from the diary of Esther Cox. August 23rd 1878

I ain't a bad girl. I don't care what anyone says. I was brought up in a right and Christian manner.

I done told Bob MacNeal that even before I got into the Surrey with him. Daniel glowered at us from the door as we rode off. He wasn't happy about me walking out with Bob, but he ain't my father. He ain't hardly five years older than me yet he treats me like a child.

Well I was eighteen on my birthday, and that surely ain't no child around these parts. Janet Briggs had a baby just last week, and she's no more than sixteen summers. There was talk at church that Bob might be the father but he has promised himself to me alone. I am his sweetheart, and he says that he loves me.

He was so sweet. He came to the door and asked for me, real proper like, and he complimented me on my new dress. When he kissed me on the cheek I felt hot all over.

He took his time driving along our street, just as I asked. Everyone was out on their porches enjoying the evening breeze, and we made sure they all saw us as we trotted out of town.

It was one of those fine late summer nights, when the air is just starting to chill and you know that Fall is right around the corner and you'd better enjoy the sun while you still can. Ain't nothing finer than sitting in a Surrey with your beau on a night like that.

Bob drove us out on the Nappan Road. At first we

passed some people, mostly folks gathering berries to make jelly for the coming winter. But soon we had the lane to ourselves and he gave the horses their head. We had a fine time bouncing and tumbling along the ruts hardened by a long hot summer.

He stopped when we came to Croziers pond. When he put his hands on my waist to lift me down it felt so sweet that I let him leave his arm around me as we sat and watched the sun go down over the water.

That is when he told me.

He loves me.

He said it real soft, scarcely more than a whisper.

His hand crept to my bosom, and I let it lie there. But I ain't no bad girl.

That evening was just the best ever. The sun went down pink and purple and Bob held me closer as the air turned chill. He whispered to me, of new dresses, of marriage. And he spoke of a house of our own where children would run. He knew just what I wanted.

So I let his hand stray across my bosom, and I did not complain when his attentions became stronger. It was only when his hand moved to my knee that I began to protest. Even then, I did not struggle too much, for if truth be told, I found pleasure in his advances.

But I ain't a bad girl. When his hand went up under my petticoat I slapped him away, hard. I done seen in his eyes that he weren't happy, but Jane had told me all about what boys would be after.

He held me some more, and whispered some more, but now it sounded cold, and the chill had settled deeper into my bones.

I told him to take me home.

And that's when it happened.

He done told me I was a *tease.* He said I was a bad girl underneath, and that he knew all about girls like me.

Then he took out his gun and told me to lie still.

He said I would enjoy it, but I didn't. Not one bit.

He ran his hands all over me underneath my skirts. His face looked red in the last of the sun's light. He looked like Old Nick himself, smiling in the fires of Hell.

So I waited until he unbuckled his trousers then did what Jane had taught me. I kicked him hard, between the legs. He moaned and fell off me. His gun fell to the ground. He made a grab for it, but he was more concerned with the thing between his legs and was slow and clumsy. He no longer looked red. His face was pale, a grey pallor that made him look half-dead. He did not look anywhere near as attractive as he had earlier on the porch.

I took the gun and raked it across his nose. Blood, black in the darkness, spurted.

Even then he did not stay down. He circled me, like a cat after a mouse. Indeed, he may have caught me, but just then I heard a carriage rattle across the ruts and I yelled, loud.

I turned my head to see who might be coming.

The gun went off, jarring my arm all the way up to my shoulder. It suddenly felt too heavy, so I dropped it to the ground. I half-expected Bob to keep coming for me, but when I looked he was dragging himself slowly up into the Surrey. He moved as if he was hurt. I guess my kick did more damage than I thought.

The next thing I remember is old man Crozier pulling me up into his wagon.

Ain't nobody seen Bob for three days now.

Despite everything I miss him.

I am his sweetheart, and he said that he loves me.

~-oOOo-~

Extract from the diary of Daniel Teed. August 23rd 1878

There is something wrong with my sister-in-law Esther. She will not say a bad word about him, but if that rascal MacNeal has harmed her in any way I swear I will swing for him.

I did not want her walking out with him in the first place, but she is as headstrong as her sister is, and I have learned long since not to get between a Cox woman and anything that she desires.

MacNeal always was going to turn out to be a bad 'un. Ever since he was a boy he has been picking fights, lighting fires and more recently whooping it up down at the saloon on a Saturday night. Then there is the matter of the Briggs girl. She swears blind that MacNeal is the father of her child, and no amount of nay-saying on his behalf will persuade me otherwise.

Good riddance to him. Old man Crozier said he saw him hightailing off in the Surrey like a rat with a squib up its arse.

He had better not come back.

~-oOOo-~

Extract from the diary of Esther Cox. September 3rd 1878

There is still no news of Bob MacNeal. I do hope he comes back. I am so sorry I hurt him. But I ain't a bad girl. I couldn't do what he wanted.

I missed the dance in the church hall on Saturday. Jane wanted me to go with her, but I waited at home to see if Bob would call on me.

The house was quiet. The parlour was too cold, too dark, so I took my book and a candle upstairs to my room. When the wind dropped I could hear the fiddles from the hall and it fair set my feet to tapping. The new dress hung behind the bedroom door, and I knew it would only take me ten minutes to dress and take myself along to the dance.

But then I might miss Bob calling at the door, and I so wanted to see him again.

So I sat still and quiet, listening for his Surrey on the road outside.

The first time I heard the mouse, if that is indeed what it was, I nearly jumped out of my skin. At first it was little more than a rustle behind the headboard. We are used to mice coming in from the fields when the temperature starts to drop. A good thump on the wall usually sends them scurrying for safety... but not this one.

The tap-tap of its feet sounded in time with the music of the dance for a second. From where I sat on the high bed I could not see it, but I heard it run along the side of the wall towards the window. I got up slowly and carried the candle over. Even as I got closer it scurried away again, and even bending down towards the floorboards I could not quite catch sight of it as it merged with the shadows.

I went back to my book but I could not concentrate. Every time I came close to losing myself in the tale, the *pitter-patter* of tiny feet would start again. I gave up trying to read and lost myself in reverie, imagining Bob and I together on the dance floor, him holding me tight and everyone watching us.

A louder scrape brought me back to myself. The cardboard box in which my dress had arrived moved across the floor and came to a halt near the door. As I got off the bed it moved again, sliding noisily back to where it had originally been standing against the wall. I watched it warily but the movement was not repeated.

I lay back and watched the moon cast shadows on the ceiling in time with the dance music wafting on the wind.

Sleep was a long time coming, and when I woke I did not feel at all rested.

~-o0O0o-~

Extract from the diary of Daniel Teed. September 3rd 1878

I know not what to make of it.

We were late in getting back from the church hall and the house was in darkness. I was slightly merry, having taken too much beer during the course of the evening, and I felt hot and tired.

All I wanted to do was fall into bed and rest.

But it was not to be.

Jane noticed the sound first, a far-off scratching, like fingernails on wood. I would have put it down to mice or maybe squirrels, but the sobbing started almost as soon as I put a foot on the stairs to the upper floor.

We found Esther lying on top of the bedclothes. She was as naked as the day she was born. Jane shooed me away, but not before I saw that her body seemed gross and bloated, like a neglected cow that has not been milked for many days. Her eyes stared at the ceiling but she did not react to our presence. She just kept sobbing in a soft piteous mewling that brought tears to all that heard it.

Jane pushed me out into the hall where my brother John stood, unsure what was to be done. We had started on our way downstairs when the whole house shook with a bang that made me think we were under attack from cannon fire. John and I ran for our guns and headed outside to meet what might be there.

There was only the clear quiet night sky.

We stood there for long minutes but there was no repeat of the noise. After a while we retired inside for some liquid courage.

Jane came down later to tell us that Esther now seemed settled and slept soundly.

In the morning Esther showed no sign of remembering any of it, and we have not spoken of it since.

~-o0O0o-~

Extract from the diary of Esther Cox. September 10th

1878

I scarce know where to begin.

My sleep has been troubled of late, and it came to a head just this last night. I tossed and turned for hours, alternatively hugging the bedclothes close to me, then throwing them asunder when they became too confining.

I had just pulled them tight around me when I heard the scampering of tiny feet once more. I intended to chase that mouse from my chamber. I threw the bedclothes off... and they kept going, sailing across the room as if propelled by a high wind. They hung, suspended in the air, a full foot above the floor.

Their crumpled shape looked like a body doubled over in pain.

I have no memory of it, but I believe I must have screamed, for I heard heavy footsteps on the stairs, and cries of concerned alarm. For my part I couldn't take my gaze from the bundle of bedclothes. It *drifted*, as if being at the whim of wind and tide. Then, just as Jane appeared in the doorway, the bundle fell to the floor with a muffled thud.

Jane and Daniel were most officious, and insisted on treating me like an invalid. Daniel made me drink a sleeping draught. It tasted vile, but within several minutes I had all but forgotten the drifting bedclothes as my mind wandered in a hazy stupor that was not unpleasant.

I have only the vaguest memory of the rest of the night, and only have Daniel's word as to what actually happened. What cannot be denied is the presence of the writing, and the whispering that I hear even now as I write this entry.

You may not believe any good of me. But if you believe nothing else, believe this.

I ain't a bad girl.

~-o0O0o-~

Extract from the diary of Daniel Teed. September 10th 1878

Esther has not been well, and things reached a climax yesterday evening.

When we arrived in the bedchamber Esther was in a state of distress, and it required a strong dose of Doctor Walton's opiates to calm her. We were about to retire, confident that the girl was now asleep, when her bedclothes blew from the bed. Esther had not moved, yet the quilt was thrown the full length of the room. When I went to retrieve it I found it to be like wrestling with a recalcitrant sheep. The material seemed to twist in my arms, fighting against me at every turn.

Brother John came to my aide. The quilt went still and we were able to drape it over Esther. But the girl was once more swollen up like a dead fish too long in the water, and her skin took on a deep red hue, as if burning from within. I dispatched John to fetch the doctor while Jane and I took turns sitting with Esther. She showed no sign of being aware of our presence, merely stared, wide-eyed and unseeing, at the ceiling.

When the doctor finally arrived, my brother John would not come back into the bedroom. Indeed, he has packed his bags and departed without saying goodbye. And I cannot say as I blame him.

The doctor had barely bent over Esther when the bedclothes swirled up as if caught by a maelstrom and wrapped themselves around the man's head, threatening to suffocate him there and then. It was only through Jane and I combining out strength that we were able to rip them from him. I thought that might be the end of his visit and that he would leave as John had left. But the doctor proved to be made of sterner stuff.

He bent forward once more and took Esther's wrist, feeling for a pulse.

At that same instant the room rang as *something* banged hard, like a child slapping his hands against the wall. The noise ran in a circle, the full turn of the room.

Then silence fell.

Esther began to thrash and moan. The banging returned, louder this time, the whole building rocking and echoing as crashes like thunder filled the room. Plaster fell from the walls and every part of my being wanted to flee, to follow my brother to the nearest inn where we could start to forget together. Only Jane's hand in mine stayed my flight.

The doctor administered laudanum and held Esther down. Slowly the drumming started to subside. Even as Esther calmed we all heard the scratching. We could not identify where it was coming from. The noise seemed to fill the air, from everywhere and nowhere.

It was Jane who saw it first. The writing appeared, scripted by an invisible hand, in crude four-inch high letters above the headboard of the bed. Just reading it made my blood run cold.

"You are mine to kill."

~-o0O0o-~

Extract from the diary of Esther Cox. October 4th 1878

The doctor said the voices would stop. Why have the voices not stopped?

Every night he drums on the walls, and every night he whispers to me, so close that I alone can hear him.

He says he loves me.

~-o0O0o-~

Extract from the diary of Daniel Teed. November 6th 1878

It is a week now since we sent Esther to the sanatorium, a week of blessed relief from that infernal drumming and the incessant scratching. The house has returned to a semblance of normality.

Esther is on the mend. The doctor says it was diphtheria, and that it will take several more weeks of rest and recuperation before she is able to return home. I am unable to reconcile the diagnosis with all that has occurred in this house, but to admit to anything other would only lead to madness.

In her delirium Esther spoke often of Bob MacNeal, and in a lucid moment told Jane that the man had tried to take advantage of her maidenhood. At that very same moment the drumming in the room reached a crescendo of noise that deafened the whole household.

I cannot help but think that all we have suffered has been a result of that night back in August. If MacNeal ever shows his face around these parts again, I shall surely kill him.

~-o0O0o-~

Extract from the diary of Esther Cox. December 14th 1878

I have only been home these past two days, yet I fear that once more I will bring terror and fear to my family.

I was so happy to be home and in my own bed again after the weeks of quiet desperation in the sanatorium. I had started to believe that the whispering had all been a delusion on my part, a reaction to the fever that had raged through me.

But the very first night home showed me that I ain't free. I might never be free again.

I was lying in my own bed, just luxuriating in the soft quilts, when I smelled smoke. Somebody laughed, a deep chuckle that sounded cold and hard. Suddenly there was heat at my feet. I had to throw the quilt to the ground and stomp on it to stop it smouldering, and if Jane ever finds out about the blackened hole there then I will be in serious trouble.

Afterwards, I found a spent match on the floor, and when I picked it up, the chuckle came again, closer this time, as if someone stood at my ear.

That was the only occurrence, but last night it happened twice – I was sitting reading quietly when once more the quilt started to burn. And even as I stomped to extinguish it, the drawer of the dresser opened and smoke came from the petticoats I have stored there.

This time I found two spent matches. As I threw the blackened stumps from the window the chuckling returned, louder this time, and with a distinct air of malice.

My heart raced, and I was unable to get any rest after that. As I lay there in the darkness the sound I had not heard in months came back – sibilant whisperings in my ear, of love and honor, of fidelity... and of death.

I am greatly afeard, but I dare not tell.

If I tell, they will surely send me away again. That is what happens to bad girls. And next time I may not be allowed to return.

~-o0O0o-~

Extract from the diary of Daniel Teed. December 26th 1878

We cannot take any more. Yuletide is meant to be a time of rejoicing and celebration. This year, our gifts were only fire and terror.

It all started so innocuously. The alarms of the autumn had been forgotten, and, while Esther was still pale and confined herself mostly to her room, there had been no incident of real note since her return these two weeks past.

I set the Yule Log to burn on the fire and nailed the holly wreaths in the porch. There had been a light snowfall overnight, and I called the family to see the scene before any thaw could tarnish it. It was an idyllic moment... but that was as good as the day ever got.

We were all on the porch when Esther started to scream – so loud that I saw lace curtains twitch and doors open all along the street as our neighbours took notice. As luck would have it I was closest to the door, and first up the stairs.

Esther sat on a bed of quilting that was already well alight, screaming as dancing flames reached for her. Jane arrived at my heels and between us we managed to drag her off the bed and away from the fire.

The flame had already taken hold in the walls, and we had to take to ferrying buckets up the stairwell. Townsfolk arrived to throw water on the exterior to prevent the fire spreading, and even then we only just managed to control the raging conflagration.

Afterwards, as we all stood outside staring at the charred side of the building, I was aware that our neighbours were being vocal in their disapproval of Esther's continued presence in the street. There was even talk of sending for a priest.

I myself had to stand between Esther and three women intent on *beating the devil out of the girl.*

Matters came round to shouting and pushing, and may have turned to something even worse had John White not intervened. He has always had a soft spot for Esther, even when she was but a child, and he has offered to take her into rooms in his inn on the other side of town, until things calm down.

Esther seems amenable to this offer, and she has gone with the innkeeper.

I spent much of my Christmas clearing up water

damage and salvaging what I can from the ruin of her room.

I am far from feeling any festive cheer.

~-o0O0o-~

Extract from the diary of Esther Cox. February 14th 1879

I had thought John White to be a friend. Indeed, I do believe his intentions to be sincere. But this table rapping smacks of the devil's business, and I ain't sure that any good will come of it.

His friends are nice people, and they mean well, but they seemed far too excited when my whispering friend decided to share his affections with them around their table. There is talk of inviting a man from the newspapers, and Mr. White whispered of visitors from as far as New York.

And I have discovered something I did not know. My whispering man has a name. Rab Nickle he calls himself, and right proud of it he seems too.

The others have not yet seen his cruelty. He pricks me with needles that can not be seen, scratches me with invisible nails. The pain is excruciating. He says I deserve it. He says that one day I will burn with him in hell.

The others think I jest when I talk like this. They do not know him as I do... they do not fear him, and the foul beings that he sometimes brings with him.

But they will come to realize the error of their ways.

I can only hope it will not be too late.

~-oOOOo-~

Extract from the diary of Daniel Teed. June 8th 1879

She is home.

Jane at least is most glad to see her sister after such an absence. And Esther herself is full of stories of *away*. Her sojourn with John White has led to a change in her, and I am not yet sure it is for the better. She says there have been no *incidents* for some months.

Indeed, she has travelled farther than any of us have, to Moncton and Halifax, St John and Fredrickstown. She seems to have spent most of her time sitting at tables and interpreting the raps that have ensued. She now says that the events of last year were due to people *from the other side* trying to communicate with her. She clearly believes herself to be communing with these spirits, and indeed John White shares these fantasies.

Esther does not seem quite herself. There is a distant quality to her that was not previously apparent, and she is pale and drawn. She wears high necked and long sleeved dresses, and will not even suffer Jane to see what is beneath, but at lunch one arm of her dress rode up and showed a mess of purple bruising and raised welts.

John White says that everything has been *normal*. However, there was a look in his eye that told a lie to that statement. I pressed him for information, and he regaled me with tales of *experiments* and even showed me some newspaper cuttings that declared Esther to be a marvel.

John White has asked my permission to invite a

certain Mr. Walter Hubbell to talk to Esther. Mr. Hubbell is deemed an *expert* on these matters... if there is indeed any such thing. But John seems to believe that the man may be able to help, and I have given my tentative agreement.

Over supper I started to wonder whether I had made the right decision. Esther barely touched her food. She seemed over-eager to get back to *her* room. We have had it redecorated for her return, and it looks just as she left it.

And that is what worries me.

Just before she retired for the night she was asking after Bob MacNeal, and whether there was any news of him. It is almost as if she still expects the man to call on her again... almost as if that is what she has been waiting for all these months.

Mr. Hubbell will be here in two months.

Let us hope he arrives before any more trouble comes our way.

~-o0O0o-~

Extract from the diary of Esther Cox. June 9th 1879

I knew as soon as I walked in the door that he was waiting for me.

He says that if I will be his bad girl, he will love me forever and never hurt me again.

~-o0O0o-~

Extract from the diary of Daniel Teed. August 18th

1879

Walter Hubbell arrived today. He may soon wish he had not bothered to make the journey.

It began as soon as he entered the house. He had barely shaken my hand when the whole upstairs of the dwelling started to reverberate with the all too familiar pounding. He followed me upstairs showing no little trepidation.

Esther was in the throes of one of her attacks. Her flesh had bloated and swelled, orange as a pumpkin and almost fit to burst. Hubbell held his umbrella ahead of him as if it were a sword he might use to protect himself.

It proved useless. An unseen force tore the umbrella from his hand and dashed it, over and over, against the dresser until it was no more than a tangle of cloth and stays. And the presence did not finish there. Hubbell's tweed trousers started to smoke – first at the ankles, then at the thighs until he was forced to divest himself of them completely. If it had not been for the raw burns raised on his skin I might have almost found it comical.

A lesser man might have taken to his heels and fled, but it seems that our Mr. Hubbell is made of stern stuff. After redressing himself he once more ventured into the room. He spoke calmly to Esther, as if addressing a distraught child, and, eventually, she did indeed calm herself.

I watched from the doorway as he whispered to her. I was too far away to hear what was being said, but from the intonation in his voice I soon realized he was asking a series of questions.

After a time *something* began to answer, manifesting itself as a series of raps on the wall... one rap for *No*, two for *Yes.*

Hubbell kept up the questioning.

Esther seemed to be sleeping soundly, but still the rapping answers echoed around the room.

Finally, after what seemed an age, Hubbell seemed satisfied. He rose and led me back down to the kitchen where I poured us both a large measure of whisky.

The man was quiet for a long time before he spoke, and when he did it was in a hushed whisper. He told me his *expertise* actually comes from the fact that he is a stage magician. He has arrived to debunk Esther's story, expecting to find fraud.

Now he believes he has found something else.

He believes she tells the truth, and that the spirits really do possess my sister-in-law.

I know not whether to be happy or appalled.

~-o0O0o-~

Extract from the diary of Esther Cox. September 12th 1879

Mr. Hubbell has been here for nearly a month now, and I scarcely remember a minute of it.

He says that we are making good progress, and that the *personalities* are providing him with a wealth of material. He intends to write a book, and says it will make our fortune.

I do not have the heart to tell him that Rab Nickle is a cheat and a liar. Mr. Hubbell is only being told what he wants to hear, and the poor man is so besotted with the notion of writing the book that he is rushing ahead regardless.

In the meantime, Rab has kept whispering to me. He really is *most* insistent. He says he will not go until I do just what he says. He tortures me nightly, with burns and pinpricks. Jane has taken to leaving pails of water around the room, and last night she caught the flames just as the drapes on the window took alight, otherwise we might all have perished.

Rab was not amused, and pricked me mightily in the thighs. He has demanded a burning, a conflagration that will sweep away all doubt. I am sorely afeard that I will give in to his insistence.

But I must remain strong. Mr. Hubbell has arranged a *soiree* for next week. He has invited dignitaries from all over and says that I will be a sensation. Rab is already whispering of it. He says that unless I do as he says, he will be very naughty indeed.

But I ain't no bad girl. I cannot do it. I *will* not do it.

~-o0O0o-~

Extract from the diary of Daniel Teed. September 20th 1879

Mr. Hubbell's stay had rather an abrupt end. He has only his own *hubris* to blame for the debacle.

The church hall was full last night and people had come from far and wide. There was even a newspaperman from Boston, sitting there in clothes better suited for a Yankee summer than a Maritime Fall.

Many of our neighbours packed the rear of the room, eager to finally get a look at the object of all their gossip.

Esther did not disappoint.

It started quietly, with more table rapping taking place in almost total darkness. The large crowd started to get restless, and indeed Tom Allardyce had to be escorted from the hall for making lewd suggestions as to what might be going on *under* the table. Mr. Hubbell remained unruffled, and at this point Esther was calm, even if her blank stare and rapid breathing was proving most disconcerting.

The in-comers at the front were rapt and stiff with attention throughout. Even more so when Hubbell had the lights lit and proceeded to demonstrate Esther's remarkable affinity with needles. I had seen her attract metal objects several times over the past months, purely by stretching her hand out for them, but Hubbell had taken this aptitude further, using his obvious stagecraft to send needles dancing in the air above the tables. He continued to amuse and entertain, even while poor Esther sat there, red as hot coals and sweating profusely. I had a mind to put a stop to the nonsense then and there, and indeed, some of the audience agreed with me. Several people left, shaking their heads, and yet others started to heckle loudly.

Alice Brown brought the evening to its abrupt end by wondering out loud what Bob MacNeal had ever seen in someone as ugly as Esther. She immediately regretted it when a needle that had just been hovering above the table flew across the hall and embedded itself in her cheek.

Things quickly went to hell in a hand basket. Hubbell had to step back sharply as the table overturned. The hall went cold, so quickly that I saw my breath condense in front of me.

The curtains on either side of the stage started to smoke and smoulder, and Esther herself convulsed, her body racked with involuntary tremors.

I leapt on stage and threw her over my shoulder, intent on carrying her away as quickly as I was able.

Stagehands were already working hard to douse a fire that had leapt up all around the hall, and as I left, Hubbell had to be soaked to avoid his expensive looking suit bursting into flame.

Esther did not wake until we got her home and into bed. Even then, she showed no memory of the night's activities.

Mr. Hubbell arrived some time later and sheepishly vacated his room. He is still convinced that he will write his book, but he does not intend to return to Amherst.

I am sure that is for the best, for all of us.

~-o0O0o-~

Extract from the diary of Esther Cox. September 21st 1879

Rab was happy with his *performance* in the church hall, and even happier to have seen off Mr. Hubbell.

He says now that he has me to himself, things will be much better.

As for myself, I discovered something very

interesting during Mr. Hubbell's time here. Yes, Rab is inside me. But when he is making his mischief, he is *outside* me.

Rab is a bad man.

And I ain't a bad girl.

But if I want to get rid of him, that might have to change.

~-o0O0o-~

Extract from the diary of Daniel Teed. October 10th 1879

Wonders will never cease.

Esther has taken employment, working for Arthur Davison out at the Barrens, looking after his livestock. And she seems to have settled into a routine.

I do believe that with Hubbell leaving, the worst of it may have gone with him.

~-o0O0o-~

Extract from the diary of Esther Cox. October 28th 1879

I am free and I have Mr. Davison's barn to thank for it.

It happened last night.

I had come prepared. The matchbox felt hot in my pocket, and I was worried that at any moment Rab would guess my intent and punish me further.

But he had other things on his mind.

I was in the barn fetching some straw for the horses

195

when Rab chose to misbehave. I only noticed when the wall opposite me quivered, the straw shaping and moulding itself, running together and binding, small knots forming as I watched. A bulge appeared in the straw, a bulge that forced itself into shape, first a head covered in flaxen hair then shoulders, tanned and golden. Rab's face leered at me.

"Be nice to me and I will love you forever," he whispered.

My hand shook violently as I tried to open the matchbox and I nearly dropped the contents when the straw *thing* that Rab inhabited reached for me. I felt a hand on my knee, attempting to reach under my petticoat.

I struck match after match and dropped them in the straw. Slowly but sure they started to take.

I knocked the straw hand away from my leg and dropped a freshly lit match on the forearm. It went up with a *whoosh*. The flames spread fast, and I had to step away to avoid being burned.

Rab laughed loudly, even as the barn took hold and the straw in which his features were etched started to break apart, sending sparks to dance in the wind.

"That's my bad girl," he whispered. "You do not need me any more."

And as simply as that, he was gone.

I retreated outside and watched the fire burn. Rab's face leered at me one last time from the raging flames before the roof collapsed and the barn fell in on itself sending sparks, and all that remained of Rab Nickle, flying and dispersing in the wind.

Afterwards they put me in a cell, and said that I

would be here for a while.

I do not care. I have been listening hard, and there have been no more whispers.

~-o0O0o-~

Extract from the diary of Daniel Teed. December 10th 1879

I cannot tell Esther. I am worried what might happen if I do. She has only just been released to our custody and although she *seems* fine, we are all still tiptoeing around her, and no one will talk of what has occurred.

They found a body out in Croziers Pond yesterday. The critters have been at it, and it cannot with any certainty be said who it might be. But it has a bullet hole in its back, and old Doc Walton says that it has been in the water for more than a year.

~-o0O0o-~

Extract from the diary of Esther Cox. December 10th 1879

I am a bad girl.
And I am free.

Dancers

Yes, I know it's getting dark, and I know it's getting cold, but just come over here for a minute. It won't take much of your time. There's something I want to show you, someone I'd like you to meet.

Come on. Humour an old man who needs to tell his secret.

It's just there, behind the church. Yes, in the older graveyard. You're not afraid are you? I promise, there's nothing here that would ever hurt you.

Not you.

Watch out for the moss on the stones. Some of the slimier varieties can get embedded in your clothes, and it's murder trying to get it out.

Just about there is usually the best spot. Stand quietly now – let your eyes get adjusted to the dark. You'll soon see why I brought you here.

There she is.

Do you see her? She's standing right there. Look – in front of the large grey angel, just to the left of the patch of moonlight, almost underneath the old elm. Yes, there, beside the largest headstone.

My beautiful Sarah. Forever young, forever twenty.

See how the red of her hair glows like a burning firebrand, a halo around the white perfection of her face. And look – she's wearing the dress. The one I bought her for the dance, the last dance of our youth.

Three pounds two and sixpence that dress cost me – more than a week's wages in those days. Times have changed, haven't they? My mother told me that I was

199

mad, spending all that money on a slip of a girl who was no better than she should be. But I knew she was worth every penny.

I was drunk with the delight that danced in her eyes when she tried it on, swaying her hips to get the full effect from the long flowing pleats. I can still remember even now, fifty odd years and many strangers' kisses later, the sweet honeyed taste of her lips as she thanked me, the pressure of her hands on my back as we embraced.

I wish she would touch me now. Just one touch, to bring us together at the end. If only she could see me. I have so much that I've never told her.

How still she is, how composed. The wind refuses to ruffle her, the rain refuses to dampen her, the earth refuses to cling to her. Yet there's something more.

Look closer. She breathes; she blinks; her lips part and then connect, but there's no steam. Not like you and I, standing here puffing at each other. It may be almost winter here, but for her it's late summer, always summer.

Those lips. How deep and red and enticing they were that night, glistening moistly as she looked up at me. Smiling, dancing, laughing, we moved across the dance floor. We were young; the war had barely touched us, and I was in love for the very first time. The night held the prospect of many new pleasures.

And then he arrived.

I knew he was going to be trouble. Right from the start I could see what he was. American, charming, arrogant and different. Hello excitement, goodbye dependability. In the space of a minute I'd lost her forever.

Shall I tell you how it happened?

He butted in on our dance. Just barged right in, excused himself, and then off they went, whirling round the floor in a flurry of legs and feet and arms. I tried to stop him as they came round again, but he had all the advantages – height, weight, diet, composure and training – while I merely had my rage.

Afterwards, as I lay there on the floor, my tongue counting teeth as my handkerchief vainly tried to soak up blood, I heard a laugh. Looking up through eyes which had already begun to puff up, I saw her. Only six feet away, but already distant, clinging to the conqueror. Her hair made a red scar where it fell on her shoulder, and in that moment I knew what I would have to do.

Can you see? She's moving. But watch. Do her legs bend? Does she walk like you or me? Or does she glide, smooth and silent like a great white owl? Listen. Can you hear any gravel being trodden underfoot? Or is there only you and me and silence?

You can't tell, can you? She deceives the brain, but doesn't brook too much attention. Try not to look too closely – set your mind on other matters.

Ah yes. The chiming. It must be eight o'clock again. Do you think she's able to hear? She'll be heading for the wall. When she reaches it she'll rest her elbows and look over there, to the field on the left, where the airfield used to be.

I remember the women, silent, waiting, listening for the sounds which would tell them that their men were coming back. They used to peel off one at a time as the planes returned, until only a few were left, watching and waiting and wondering.

See how the moonbeams dance around her, making her glow. So white, so brilliant, so pure. And no shadow to taint the vision.

He was corrupting her. I could see that, even from the few glimpses I had of them together. There they were, laughing and giggling like a pair of kids fresh out of school. And kissing! In public! Right there on the main street for all too see, and again, later, in the pub, flaunting themselves in front of me.

Of course she had stockings. And lipstick. And chocolate. And cigarettes. The price of her innocence, the wages of sin.

I hoped that I wouldn't be too late, that she was still capable of being saved. I watched. I waited. I planned. He continued with her destruction, but soon I'd have my turn.

See how she moves between the stones, not attempting to pass through them. Does she look solid to you? You can't see through her, not like in the books or the films. Do you think that if I went over there and put out my hand she'd be able to take it, be able to feel? Would she notice that I was there?

I have often, over the years, thought about why she returns. It is only now, when I'm near my own end, that I'm able to look at it dispassionately. Maybe, when I go to join her, we'll both understand.

Did you know that I used to be a mechanic? Well I was, and a good one at that. It was easy. I already had the run of the airfield, so it was simple to wangle myself in on the servicing of his plane. Once I had spent five minutes aboard, it was only a matter of waiting for the next flight.

I was subtle though. I didn't want the plane blowing up over land; not over England anyway. My work might have been noticed. No, the explosion would occur only when the plane climbed to more than one thousand feet. That should do it. By the time it reached that height it would be well out over the channel.

He took it out the very next day.

Look. She's reached the wall. See how her elbows stay white, despite the damp and moss and stone? Her eyes will be moist. Will those tears be real? Could I perhaps touch them? Touch them and somehow feel her pain?

The next day I saw the flight take off, twelve planes slowly gathering in formation before beginning their long climb into the sky. I watched them until they rose into the clouds, then listened as they droned away. Was there an explosion? Did the droning lessen? I never did find out.

Whether I'm a murderer or not, he never came back, and I never lost the guilt.

Later that day, when the sky was once more filled with sound, the women left the wall, one by one, until she was the only one remaining, trying to pierce the clouds as she peered avidly eastwards, willing him to return.

I stood, just about here, and watched, cursing her for her devotion, cursing him for his hold on her, as darkness fell and the skies grew silent.

It was late summer, and the temperature was dropping rapidly. A light drizzle began to fall, chilling me to the bone.

And still she waited, and still I watched.

See it. There's the cigarette. How ungainly it looks in those pearl white fingers. It burns – there's a good quarter of an inch of ash on the end – but there's no smoke, no smell.

He started her off on that habit. She'd told me that morning that she did it because it made her look like a real lady. As if she'd not been a lady before that. It made me angry, so angry that I could watch no longer.

See how she turns, surprised. Now she'll look confused for a second. Then she'll see that it's only me; only the young, fresh faced, solid, dependable me.

Watch closely now. You may just catch the disappointment as it flits across her face. Look, she turns her back again, returns to her vigil.

One look and I was consigned to despair. I grabbed her by the shoulder and pulled her around to face me, demanding that she explain herself. She struggled in my arms but I held on as we moved around in a parody of a waltz; held her as she screamed, her once-beautiful lips contorted in rage.

She pulled away once more, and this time she was too strong for me to hold on to her. Surprised to be free so easily, she lost her balance.

I reached out desperately for her as she fell, slowly, slowly, towards the unyielding gravestones. And then came the sound, the one I hear late at night in my dreams, the sound of her neck as it broke.

So now we wait, she for a sweetheart who will never return, me for an end to the guilt and the hope of forgiveness. Which of us is more dead?

And the time passes and I watch, every night, as she dances, just for me.

The Brotherhood of the Thorns

James Menzies climbed.

His fingers hurt from gripping the dry stone, and dust filled his mouth and nostrils such that even his spit felt gritty. Small stones pattered on his head from above. When he looked up he could see the earl, five yards ahead and accelerating up the face of the cliff, his prize in sight.

I just hope it is worth it.

They had been two months in the desert, dying slowly. Of the thirty men in the band that had left Jerusalem, only eight remained, and two – John the Swift, and David of Hawick – were unlikely to last another day.

All in the pursuit of something that may not exist, and may not be of any help if it does.

But the earl had been adamant. Jerusalem was fallen to the Saracens, and only a great relic could once more unite the fractured and disillusioned brethren of Christendom.

During the last days in the city, the earl had become fervent in his faith. Before the walls of the city he had smote Saladin's men with a cold rage that was frightening to behold. When the city fell he refused to go with the others to the harbours.

Instead he called for the quest. Menzies and the other men of Melrose had a mind to rebel. Ships were leaving, for Acre then for home. Following a madman through the desert after a mythical object paled by comparison. But rebellion would only be met by death.

As thralls to their Lord, they had no choice but to follow him, to whatever doom might be waiting.

And doom there had been – a searing doom in the sand as first horses, then men, buckled under the heat.

"Tell me again, Sire," Menzies had said as they left John the Miller behind, face down in the sand. "What is it that you seek?"

The earl's smile hadn't instilled any confidence.

"A relic of our Lord," the big man replied.

"You could have had them a plenty in Jerusalem, Sire," Menzies said, laughing. "I was offered enough pieces of wood from the Cross to build a boat, and enough of the Lord's finger bones such that I could give one to every man in the garrison."

The earl frowned.

"I am not talking about market baubles. I'm talking abot a major relic. Something that will unite the faith under its banner."

"Surely, if such a thing existed, it would have been found by now?"

The big man's frown grew deeper, the sign of an impending storm. In the three years since they left Melrose, a peppering of grey had grown in the earl's beard, but he was still as broad as a bear, and near as quick to anger. Menzies knew better than to push for more information.

He was not confident of the quest's success, even from the first day. Rumours of relics were a daily topic of conversation in the old city, especially once Saladin's siege began. Knights dug up large areas around the old temples in a frantic search for talismans. Indeed, it was rumoured that three French Lords had found *something* in the stables under Solomon's temple, but they were spirited away that very same night, and if they had found anything, it proved worthless against the might of the Saracen army.

Surrender had been inevitable. But the earl refused to be bowed. Even as the Saracens broke through the gates Menzies had found him in the dungeon beneath the garrison with a hot iron in his hand, standing over the body of a broken man. The earl smiled broadly at Menzies.

"It lies to the east," he said. "Across the desert to the mountains. My destiny waits there."

~-o0O0o-~

And now the earl was speeding towards that destiny, climbing towards the tower on a high crag that had been their goal these sixty days.

Menzies dragged himself up onto a ledge to find the earl contemplating the remainder of the climb. The tower was still high above them, and, although they had started in the dawn hours, the sun was already high in the sky, the heat from the rocks threatening to bake them alive.

"We must rest, Sire," Menzies said. He looked down to where the remainder of the men formed a spaced-out line of climbers, the leader of which was still some twenty yards below. "It is folly to climb in this heat."

The Earl looked up the cliff then back down at the rest of his men. He wiped sweat from his brow.

"Mayhap you are right for once," he said. "Let us find some shelter."

For the rest of the afternoon the eight men took turns in a small area of shade in a crack in the rock. John the Swift expired from his exertions as the sun began its descent far to the west, but the Earl scarcely noticed.

"Think on it, Menzies," he said, staring out over the sunset. "We could return to Jerusalem with an army at our back and a relic of the Lord before us. All of Christendom would follow. We will drive the heathen from our holy places, and ensure we keep them Christian for all time. Think of the glory of it."

Menzies was indeed thinking.

The Lord's glory? Or yours?

The stars began to show overhead.

"Come, lads," the Earl said. "One last push, and we shall have our reward."

He faced the cliff and started to climb, not once looking back. The broadsword slung across his shoulders *clanged* against the rock, but if the Earl worried about giving away their position, he did not show it, merely climbed faster.

The remaining men shouldered whatever packs and weapons they carried and, with heavy hearts, followed.

Menzies decided to bring up the rear. David of Hawick seemed near his end, and it would be a wonder if he could make this last stretch of the climb. Menzies cajoled him every inch of the way, reminding him of the rolling hills and forests of home, of damp foggy days and welcome cold winds. Much to Menzies' surprise, the man made it to the top, hauling himself, panting, over a lip.

They found the Earl and the other four men standing in a small clearing before a tall tower. The tower was unremarkable, a three-level block of sandstone heavily weathered by the elements, so old that it almost looked like part of the cliff itself. In the gathering gloom the darkened windows seemed like empty, unstaring eyes and Menzies felt a chill run through him that had nothing to do with the encroaching night.

The Hawick man had to sit almost immediately, all strength gone from his body. The others aside from the Earl looked in little better shape, their faces drawn and haggard, shoulders slumped with fatigue.

"We must rest, Sire," Menzies said. "If there's fighting to be done this night, we won't last more than a minute. The men can barely lift their arms, never mind a weapon."

The Earl didn't answer at first. He stood staring at the tower, his eyes in shadow, the black holes mirroring the windows in the building.

"It is there," he whispered. "We are close. I can feel it."

It was obvious to Menzies that his sire was like a horse champing at the bit, eager to surge forward and find what waited for him in the tower. But in the end he relented, allowing the men a few hours respite.

They sat in the clearing in front of the tower, in plain sight of anyone who might be watching, eating what meagre rations remained to them. The Hawick man produced a tinder-box and with that and the aid of some dead wood they managed to get a small fire burning.

No one spoke, each man lost in his own thoughts.

If anyone in the tower paid them any attention they did not show it. The dark shadows in the windows grew black as full night fell. A crescent moon rose above them and the desert sky blazed in a milky sea of stars. Still no one appeared from the tower, or showed themselves at the windows. There was no sound save their own breathing.

"The place seems empty, Sire," one of the men said.

The Earl rose. Chain mail rustled. Menzies was amazed that the big man had got up the cliff wearing it. The rest of them had ditched theirs in the sand in favour of leather tunics and desert robes, swapping their longswords for smaller, lighter blades that were more easily carried in the searing heat. But the Earl refused to bow completely to the elements. Although he had ditched most of his armour, he retained the mail beneath a long heavy tunic and had carried the heavy sword all the way from Jerusalem. Now he unsheathed it from its scabbard. Moonlight glinted along the blade. Once more the mail rustled.

He must have been near to baking inside there.

But still he'd been the one pushing them all the way, and the first, and fastest man, up the sheer cliff face.

"The Lord wills it," was all he had ever said when pushed on the matter.

Now the big man stood staring at the tower, and Menzies knew exactly where the *Lord's will* was going to lead them next.

The big man turned to Menzies, and for a second a shadow of fear seemed to slide across his features.

"If I should fall, bury me at home, Menzies. Promise me that at least?"

Menzies nodded.

"I have always served you, Sire. I will serve in this matter, too."

The Earl nodded.

"Then come. Let us see if the truth was told in yon dungeon in Jerusalem."

~-o0O0o-~

The Earl went first. Behind him the others drew their swords and kept close order. Menzies brought up the rear with David of Hawick. The man leaned on his sword, using it as a walking stick.

"Stay here, man," Menzies said. "No one will think the less of you."

The Hawick man laughed, his voice little more than a whisper.

"And let you Melrose men get all the glory? I'd never be able to show my face at home again. Come. Let us see what wonders our liege has led us to."

The two of them were several yards behind the others as they approached the main entrance to the tower. It had been in deep shadow earlier, but as they approached they saw that a thick wooden door protected the doorway. It was currently closed.

The Earl banged hard on it with the hilt of his sword.

"There are Christian men here seeking succour," he shouted, his voice echoing in the cliffs.

All fell quiet for the space of five heartbeats, then the door swung open. Around Menzies the men gripped harder at their swords.

The Earl had the longsword raised high above his head, ready for any attack, but lowered it when a hooded figure in long grey robes appeared in the doorway. The hood fell forward over the man's face, obscuring his features in shadow. The only distinguishing mark on the robes was a black circle, crudely painted on at the chest. The robe trailed on the ground so that not even his feet were visible, and his hands were lost in swathes of material that fell in voluminous folds over his arms.

The men did not relax, but there seemed to be no attack forthcoming. The grey robed figure just stood there, blocking the door.

"We are Christian men needing shelter and succour," the Earl said again. "Will you let us enter?"

The grey figure stood still and silent.

"Let us enter," the Earl said, raising his voice. Menzies knew that anger was near the surface now.

The grey figure did not respond.

"Are you daft, man?" the Earl said, and stepped forward.

The robed figure raised a hand and placed it against the Earl's chest. It seemed innocuous enough, little more than a warning gesture. But the Earl pressed forward, straining. No matter how much effort he put into the act, he was unable to force himself past the man, unable to move the hand from its place on his chest.

Still the grey figure did not speak.

"You cannot refuse me," the Earl shouted. "I do the Lord's will."

He stepped back and hacked at the offending arm with a downward blow of the longsword.

There was a dull *thud.*

Menzies looked to the ground, for by rights, that was where the arm should lie. The stroke should have cleaved it from the body.

The grey figure had not moved as the sword came down. There was a long cut in the robe, and beneath it pale wrinkled flesh showed.

There is no wound. Barely even a scratch.

The Earl raised the sword again. Before he could bring it down the grey figure stepped forward under the blade. A white hand grabbed at the Earl's tunic and, with as little effort as a child tossing a pebble, threw the Earl backward to land heavily on his hind-end in the dust.

Beside Menzies, the Hawick man started to pray.

The grey figure withdrew his hand back into the robes and stood, silent and still in the doorway.

The Earl struggled to his feet.

"Kill him," he shouted.

The four men in front of Menzies raised their swords and attacked. The grey figure let them come. He caught the first swinging sword with his left hand, gripping the blade tight.

There is no blood.

With a tug the robed man pulled the attacker off balance and caught him, one-handed, around the throat. He twisted. The snap of the man's neck breaking echoed in the hills above them. Another of the Earl's men fell to the ground. The grey figure stomped on his back, foot crushing all the way through his spine with a crack of bone and a gush of blood that soaked the bottom foot of the robe.

"They are devils," the Hawick man said. "We cannot fight such as these."

"We have the Lord on our side," the Earl said and

pushed past Menzies. "We shall prevail."

The two men left in the doorway rained blow after blow on the robed thing before them. Bits of cloth flew. Where the blades found their mark they made only a dull thud, like striking wood instead of flesh.

One of the men overreached with a blow. The grey one swatted the sword aside and thrust a hand into the man's chest, punching all the way through the ribs and out the man's back. Blood sprayed, and Menzies tasted it in his mouth.

It sent the Earl into a frenzied attack.

The last of the four men who had pressed the attack fell away from the doorway, dead eyes staring accusingly at Menzies.

The Hawick man tugged at Menzies' tunic. "Come away, James. This is madness," he said.

But Menzies could not take his eyes from the Earl. The big man pressed an attack with the longsword that would have felled many Saracens in battle, moving fluidly and swiftly, raining blow after blow on the grey figure.

The air was filled with the sound of sword strokes thudding into the body beneath the robes.

Yet still it stood.

"Die you devil, die!" the Earl shouted. "In the name of our Lord Jesus Christ."

The grey figure went still. It raised its head, as if listening. The hood of the robe fell back from its face, revealing a pale ivory visage. Milk-white eyes stared blindly at the Earl. Its mouth opened and closed, revealing yellow teeth and a grey tongue inside, but no sound came. It made no defence as the Earl brought the sword round in one clean sweep that nearly took its head off at the neck.

The body fell to the ground and lay still.

Menzies relaxed his grip on his sword. He hadn't even had a chance to swing it.

~-o0O0o-~

The Earl stood over the robed figure.

"Let us see what manner of thing this is."

He bent and pulled the robe away.

The body below was thin to the point of emaciation, ribcage showing through skin that was almost translucent. The milky-white eyes stared from lidless sockets and when Menzies bent to check the body, the hair felt dry as straw. He touched a cheek. The flesh was cold, but not overly so. It felt too stiff, too unyielding. He rapped his knuckles on an arm. It rang, like a piece of wood.

"What devilry is this?"

"That is not all," the Earl said. "Look."

He held up one of the grey figure's hands. The fingernails were long and pointed, with a deep brown hue that shone in the moonlight where it caught on razor sharp edges.

"Have you ever seen anything like it, Hawick?" Menzies said.

When there was no reply he looked around.

David of Hawick was nowhere to be seen.

The Earl clapped Menzies on the shoulder.

"Never fear, lad. We two are enough for any foe. We have the Lord on our side. Come. Our destiny awaits us."

Menzies followed the Earl into the tower.

~-o0O0o-~

The doorway led into a large open area. There were carvings, and carved pillars, everywhere Menzies looked.

One particular pillar caught his eye. Some eight feet tall and nearly two feet wide, the carvings ran up its length in a loose spiral. Red serpents lay at its base, and dark bat-winged fiends circled its top. In the spiral carving, men screamed in torment as demons fed.

"A pretty place for worship," the Earl said at his side.

Another set of carvings caught his eye; a naked figure, blindfolded, with cherub's wings but milky-white eyes. It had one hand on its breast, and another on its right calf. A grey figure, also blindfolded, hung suspended upside down in a tight coil of rope, and a cherub, paler than the rest, sucked hungrily from a bloody heart, while the heart's owner looked on in horror.

"What are we looking for?" Menzies whispered. "For I would like to find it quickly, and leave this place."

The Earl did not reply. He started to make his way around the chamber, tapping on the stone with the hilt of his sword, looking for hidden spaces.

For the next half an hour they searched the chamber, but there was only the stone and the carvings.

Outside the moon went behind a cloud and the

gloom deepened such that it was almost impossible to make out anything beyond the position of the exterior doorway and the high windows.

"We cannot stay," Menzies whispered. "There may be more of those grey demons here somewhere. In this darkness it would be folly to attempt such a thing."

The Earl nodded.

"It will be dawn soon enough, and we will return."

They made for the door, but never reached it. The moon threw shadows across the threshold as four tall grey figures came inside. Menzies recognised them immediately despite their milky-white stares. The last time he'd seen them they'd been lying on the ground dead. Even in the gloom he could make out the bloody hole in the chest of the first through the door.

~-o0O0o-~

On the far side of the chamber a section of the wall slid aside, stone grating against stone. Someone stood in the new doorway, backlit by flickering torches beyond. This one was taller by a hand than any of the others, and wore a white robe, but still with the crude black circle emblazoned on the chest. He raised an arm.

The four figures at the doorway came forward, slowly, deliberately.

Menzies and the Earl moved so that they stood back to back.

"We're in a tight spot, Sire," Menzies said.

"Near as bad as yon whorehouse in Nicosia," the Earl replied.

They were still laughing when the first of the four

moved forward to attack.

Seconds later Menzies was fighting for his life, against men who had been his companions just an hour before, men who showed no recognition, just stared at him from dead white eyes.

The Earl was able to keep his two at bay by using the length of the longsword to his advantage, but Menzies struggled. His sword was good for close quarters, for stabbing opponents in their soft tissues at stomach and groin. But the things that attacked him were far from soft.

A cold hand grabbed him at the left bicep and started to squeeze. The pain sent white heat lancing through Menzies. He threw himself away to one side, lashing out with the sword as he hit the ground. A lucky blow caught his attacker behind the knee, hobbling him and bringing the body crashing to the floor. The Earl was quick to spot the opportunity. The longsword took the head off at the neck.

"Don't get up," the Earl shouted, whirling the sword around him at head height. "You hamstring them, I'll do the rest."

The plan proved more effective than Menzies could have hoped. The grey things were strong, but seemed to lack any intelligence. Even as one fell, cut through the calf, another stepped forward within easy reach. It was hard work, and the sword had grown heavy, his arm jarred from the weight of blows necessary to get the job done.

Minutes later Menzies stood beside the Earl. They were both breathing heavily, but neither had taken a serious injury. Four bodies, twice dead now, lay at their feet. Menzies gave the nearest a hefty kick in the ribs. It didn't move.

"I think its dead. I have taken its head off," the Earl said laughing.

Menzies kicked the body again.

"And it has a hole in its chest you can see straight through. That didn't slow it down much."

The Earl kicked one of the heads. It rolled away across the floor towards the opening where the newcomer had stood. Menzies' gaze followed the path of the rolling head. The doorway was empty. Firelight flickered beyond, but there was no other movement, no other sound.

"What say you," the Earl asked, "shall we finish what we came to do?"

Menzies hefted his sword.

"After you, my lord."

~-oOOo-~

The chamber beyond was obviously the reason the tower had been built in this place. It was a vast natural cavern in the side of the cliff, the torchlight sending shadows dancing overheard until they merged with the darkness above, where the ceiling was too high to be seen in the gloom. On the far side of the cavern, some thirty paces away, the white robed figure stood in front of a plain wooden cross that towered high over him. Beside the cross sat a stone plinth. Something lay on top of the stone, but Menzies was as yet too far away to make out what it was.

The floor between the men and the cross was laid out

in a huge circular mosaic, a pattern that spiralled in towards the centre. Latin inscriptions ran alongside miniature figures. Menzies had no schooling, but the Earl had spent many a year in the cloisters of the Abbey with the monks. The Earl started to walk the spiral, mumbling to himself.

"Calgary... our Lord... King of the Jews. A storm... a crown for the king. He dies..."

Menzies got another cold chill up his spine. Suddenly he had no desire to see what lay on the plinth.

The Earl kept mumbling.

"The crown is taken, spirited away... a safe place, high in the mountains... "

He was almost at the centre of the spiral now.

"The Brotherhood of the Thorn... guardians."

He reached the centre of the spiral. He looked at his feet, then at the black circle painted on the white robe.

"I know what it is," he whispered.

He motioned Menzies over to join him. Menzies looked down.

A crown of thorns.

The Earl stared rapt, at the stone plinth.

"The crown worn by our Lord during his passion," he said. "The thorns are stained with his blood."

He turned back to Menzies.

"With this, we can retake the Holy City. With the Lord's blood in our hands, we can wipe the heathen from the face of the earth. We can make the world Christian."

Before Menzies could naysay him the Earl strode across the floor towards the plinth.

The hooded figure stepped in front of him, blocking

his path. The Earl didn't hesitate. He raised the sword and swung, backhanded. The robed figure seemed to move languidly, only raising an arm in defence. The sword went halfway through the forearm. The figure made no sound. And there was no blood. The wound gaped, grey and dry.

The Earl hacked again. The arm came away at the shoulder. The other hand gripped the sword and without seeming to exert any force, snapped it off, a foot from the hilt.

Menzies started to move forward to his liege's aid. At the same moment six more robed figures emerged from the shadows, and moved quickly to block any move he might make. They did not attack him... they didn't have to. He could not reach the Earl.

The white robed figure had the Earl by the throat. The pair spun around in a grotesque parody of a dance. The Earl was trying, without much success, to reach a vital organ with what remained of the sword. His face had gone bright red and he gasped, struggling for breath.

Menzies jumped forward, intent on trying to get through. An arm, heavy and solid, swung and hit him in the chest. It felt like he'd just ran into a tree. He went down hard, the back of his head smacking against the mosaic. His vision blurred.

His head rang like a bell, but beneath that he heard the Earl call out.

"I am here in the name of Jesus Christ. I do the Lord's will."

The white robed figure went still, staring straight at the Earl. The big man took his opportunity. He shoved the broken sword under the robed man's chin, pushing through till the blade punched out the back of the skull. The body went down without another sound.

The Earl stepped up to the plinth.

"We have it, Menzies," he shouted. He reached down towards the crown of thorns. "I have my prize."

The six robed men, as one, turned and moved towards him.

The Earl still had his back to them and did not see them approach, still intent on the crown.

"My Lord," Menzies called, but his voice was barely a whisper. He tried to stand but his legs refused to bear him. He could only watch as the six men grabbed the Earl. They took the sword from him as easily as taking a toy from a babe. Once the Earl was disarmed two of them moved aside to the large wooden cross and lowered it, almost reverentially to the ground. The others started to drag the struggling man towards it.

Menzies saw their intent and went cold.

"No!" he called, but yet again only a whisper emerged. He began to crawl forward, but his head felt like it might explode. His world began to go black at the edges.

The robed figures spread the Earl's arms along the spars of the cross.

An arm went up and came down.

There was a dull thud, then silence for a heartbeat before the Earl's screams began and a splash of red on the wood showed where he had been nailed through the wrist. The big man screamed again as it was repeated on the other side, and mercifully lost consciousness for a time as they drove a nail through both his ankles and deep into the main stay of the cross.

A figure broke away from the group to go to the plinth. It returned with the crown. The Earl woke. His eyes went wide with fear as he realized his fate. He threw his head from side to side but they held him, as if calming a recalcitrant babe. They rammed the crown down hard on the Earl's scalp. Blood joined tears to run in runnels down his face.

They hoisted the cross into place against the cavern wall.

The six figures prostrated themselves on the ground as the Earl cried out, his pain echoing around the cavern and sending bats scattering overhead.

Menzies tried to crawl, but the darkness was even closer now.

He saw the Earl raise his face to the roof and scream in pain.

"I do the Lord's will."

Soon the darkness covered even that sight. He let it take him, and fell into oblivion.

~-o0O0o-~

He woke to a headache that pounded like a drum. When he tried to stand his stomach heaved and he brought up what little he had in his stomach. After that, he felt strangely stronger.

The feeling of wellbeing only lasted as long as it took him to turn to face the cross.

The Earl hung limply – chin lowered to his chest. Blood showed all around his head where vicious thorns had pierced the scalp. More blood coated his left side from a wound that had been punched through the chain mail under his ribs. A black circle was painted on his tunic. He did not look to be breathing.

The six robed men still knelt on the ground at the foot of the cross.

My Leige!

Menzies stumbled across the cavern floor. His sword lay near the centre of the mosaic but he paid it no heed as he approached the cross.

Did the Lord will this blasphemy?

The kneeling figures ignored him as he approached. He reached up to touch the Earl's tunic.

The big man's head lifted.

He lives. My liege lives.

The Earl's eyes opened.

There were no pupils, just a blank, milky white stare.

Wood creaked and groaned. Menzies couldn't take his eyes from the face, but was aware that one wrist was now free of the nail that had pierced it. He felt gentle hands push him aside.

The robed figures helped the Earl down from the cross then prostrated themselves before him.

The Earl stood in front of the bloodstained cross and opened his arms wide. He spoke – his voice a dry rasp.

"To Jerusalem. The Lord wills it."

The kneeling figures kissed his robe.

Menzies turned and fled.

He had no idea where he was headed. He only knew that he had to get out of that chamber, away from those milky white stares.

If I had stayed there but a minute longer, I would have been tempted to join him.

He ran, slamming into the stone by the doorway. He reached the exterior door before he realized he could see clearly. The sun was rising, a thin watery dawn.

We have been in there all night.

He staggered out to the clearing. A figure loomed in front of him. He threw a punch but it didn't have strength enough to land. Someone grabbed him beneath the arms as he fell, off-balance.

"Dear God, James," David of Hawick said. "What has become of you?"

~-o0O0o-~

A minute later he was sat by the fire at the far end of the clearing. His gaze rarely left the entrance to the tower, but nothing moved there.

Not yet.

The Hawick man fed him some dried bread and wine and the heat of the fire started to loosen the chill in his bones.

"I'm sorry," David said. "I ran when I should have been by your side."

Menzies waved him aside.

"We all should have ran," he said quietly. "Mayhap we would all yet be alive."

"The Earl?"

Menzies wasn't ready to tell that story.

"What have you been doing all this time?" he asked the Hawick man.

The man looked sheepish.

"I started to run," he said. "I even got as far as going down the cliff. Then I came to the ledge where we left

John the Swift. He was just lying there, two crows feasting on his face. I couldn't find it in myself to leave him. So I made a cairn and buried him under it. I sat with him through the night, saying the words. It was the Christian thing to do."

The Christian thing to do.

Menzies sat for long minutes looking into the flames. Pictures came to mind, of the Earl, crowned in thorns, riding at the head of a vast army before the gates of Jerusalem, every man among them staring ahead with a milky-white gaze as they hacked the Saracens to bloody pieces.

And it wouldn't stop there.

He saw the Earl sitting on a throne as all the Kings of Christendom were brought before him to bend a knee, a Christendom that would all bow before the holy relic, believing it to be the Lord's will. He saw countries fall. He saw home, and Melrose Abbey, the monks in grey robes, black circles painted on their chests. He saw a world of nothing but obedience and dead white stares.

And with that came a memory of the night before.

The air is filled with the sound of sword strokes thudding into the body beneath the robes.

Yet still it stands.

"Die you devil, die!" the Earl shouts. "In the name of our Lord Jesus Christ."

The grey figure goes still. It makes no defence as the Earl brings the sword round in one clean sweep that nearly takes its head off at the neck.

Swift on the heels of that came another memory.

He hears the Earl call out.

"I am here in the name of Jesus Christ. I do the Lord's will."

The white robed figure goes still, staring straight at the Earl. The big man takes his opportunity. He shoves the broken sword under the robed man's chin, pushing through till the blade punches out the back of the skull. The body goes down without another sound.

"It was the same both times," Menzies whispered. "They made no defence."

He came to a decision. He stood, groaning at aches and pains the length of his body.

"Where to James?" David asked. "Do we head for home?"

"Not yet. Come with me, or stay, it makes no mind to me. But we have our duty as Christians to perform."

Menzies tore long strips from his tunic, and wound them tight round a piece of wood. He lit it from the fire. David of Hawick followed his example.

Together they strode back into the tower.

~-o0O0o-~

The earl and his disciples still stood before the bloodied cross, heads bowed in a mockery of prayer. The Hawick man would have ran again then, but Menzies put out a hand to stop him.

"You did right by John the Swift. Now we shall do right by our liege."

Menzies strode across the mosaic. His foot kicked his sword that still lay there, sending it skittering across the polished stone. He didn't bend to retrieve it.

I don't need it. I have something else that will serve

229

me better.

The earl looked up at his approach. The pale eyes seemed to stare into Menzies' soul. The big man opened his arms wide, welcoming.

"You have been by my side these many years," the big man said. His voice sounded dry and hoarse, and had withered to little more than a whisper. "Join me now. The Lord wills it."

"Aye," Menzies said. "The Lord wills it."

He stepped forward and thrust the burning brand into the cloth of the earl's robe. The black paint on the front took first, raising a fiery circle that spread quickly. Menzies smelled the acrid tang of burning hair as the earl's beard blazed. The big man started to flap his arms, attempting to put out the flame.

"In the name of Jesus Christ, be still," Menzies shouted.

Despite the flames, the earl complied. He stood, silent even as fire ravaged his face. The last Menzies saw was one of the white eyes pop and sizzle, then the body fell away to the ground. The disciples swayed like drunkards.

The crown of thorns hissed and crackled as the flame reached it.

The robed disciples moved forward, but even as they reached with longing towards the earl, the fire took completely and raged through the tinder-dry wood of the crown. As a man, the disciples fell, pole-axed, onto the mosaic.

~-o0O0o-~

They let the fire take its course. By the time it was done the earl's body was charred and ravaged, the crown of thorns indistinguishable from the rest of the remains.

"In the name of Jesus Christ, be at peace," Menzies said softly. He ground his foot on the remains, scattering the crown, and most of the earl's head, to dust and ash.

Just as he was leaving he remembered his promise.

Bury me at home, Menzies. Promise me that at least?

"We are a long way from there, Sire," he whispered. "But I will do what I can."

He gathered the ashes and collected them in a small leather pouch he normally used for coins. Without another word he turned and left. He did not look back.

It was only when they were back out in the heat of the sun that David of Hawick spoke.

"What did we just do?" he asked.

Menzies set his eyes on the horizon and home. He didn't reply, but something that the Hawick man had said earlier echoed in his mind.

It was the Christian thing to do.

The Young Lochinvar

Julia really wanted to see a *real* Scotchman.

Edinburgh had been a *big* disappointment. Sir Walter Scott had led her to believe there would be cultured men in fine lace and kilts, young Lochinvars ready to sweep her off her feet and dance her away to a romantic retreat where she would be smothered in soft kisses. Instead all she got was grey streets, fog and the taste of stale beer on a drunkard's lips.

Maybe Dundee will be better.

The signs were not proving good so far. The train clattered through a dark windy night that caused the carriages to sway alarmingly like a boat tossed by the waves. The sound assaulted her ears, and she yearned for the peace and quiet of their Chelsea drawing room. Pater only made things worse with his constant prattling about guns and shooting. When the other men in the carriage lit up their briar pipes in unison, Julia excused herself and left for the relatively clearer air in the corridor.

She hoped for a view from a window, something to raise her spirits, a glimpse of some *real* Scotchmen, or even some of the scenery on the subject of which Scott had waxed so eloquently. But night had fallen since the train departed Edinburgh, and any excitement Julia might have got at crossing the Forth was lost in the rain and dark. Nothing could be seen beyond the window but grey, interspersed with rivulets of water where rain splashed and was smeared by the wind.

Welcome to Scotland.

She had only thought it, but a dark figure standing where the carriages met turned towards her. He stood with a light behind him and his features lay in dark shadow. All she could tell was that he was tall, and dressed in what looked like an expensive woolen overcoat.

"Your first time here, miss?"

His voice was soft, almost timid, but Julia felt heat rising at her cheeks.

He's a Scotchman.

Yet again, although she had not spoken, he seemed to guess her intent.

"That would be *Scotsman,*" he said. "But no, I am only a visitor here."

"As am I," Julia replied, amazed at her own boldness. She looked back to the carriage. Pater was watching her closely, but he would not be able to see this stranger from where he sat.

If I keep my back to the carriage, Pater will never even know I am speaking.

"And how do you like this country?" the tall man said. His voice sounded somewhat muffled, as if coming from a much further distance.

"I like what I have seen of it just fine," she replied. "But I wish this dashed rain would ease."

"I like the rain," the man said. "And the wind. It reminds me that I am but a servant of the elemental, not a master."

What he said next was obscured as the train blasted through a short tunnel, but it had sounded like a series of numbers, ending in five and seventy.

"I'm sorry," she said. "I did not catch that."

He didn't reply, merely stood stock still. Although she could not see his eyes she felt his gaze on her like a physical force, and once again she blushed.

Her embarrassment quickly turned to confusion as the man spoke again.

"Five and seventy, three score and fifteen, a long span come to a sudden end, as they all do, in darkness and turmoil. It's coming yet, for a' that."

She might have been so bold as to question the man about his meaning, but at that moment a conductor arrived in the corridor to check tickets, and when she turned back there was no sign of the tall stranger. She considered walking through to the next carriage to see where he had gone, but she knew if she left Pater's line of sight, for even a second, it would be noted and a reprimand would not be long behind.

She went reluctantly back in to join her pater's party. For almost an hour she kept a close eye on the corridor, but the tall man did not reappear. By the time the train stopped at Kirkcaldy she had almost given up hope.

Her dismay was doubled when three young men in tweeds and plus fours boarded and Pater invited them in to the carriage.

"Julia," he said as a youth with an overbite and a terrible case of acne sat opposite her. "I would like you to meet George Kerr. His father works with me in the city. He is to be your husband."

At first she thought she had misheard, but the look in Pater's eye told her he was deadly serious. She knew better than to make a scene in company, and forced herself to sit through George's, frankly embarrassing, attempts to prove his worth.

"I am so glad to finally meet you," the youth said. His voice, when compared to the gentle softness of the man in the corridor, felt like razors in her ears. "Your father has told me all about you."

Oh, I do hope not.

"Have you been on this line before?" he asked, and continued without waiting for a reply. "It's a marvel of modern engineering. Our fathers helped build it you know?"

And without waiting again, he kept on flapping his lips. Julia tuned him out as he spent ten minutes telling her how much iron, stone and manpower went into the building of the new bridge at Dundee, the biggest, longest and most expensive ever built, and how an American president no less had called it *'a big bridge for a small city.'* That remark caused much hilarity among George and his companions, leading them to bray like excited horses.

I cannot marry such as this. But what am I to do? I must follow my pater's guide in these matters.

"We shall be at the bridge in thirty minutes or so," George said. "Isn't it exciting?"

Julie couldn't think of a suitable reply that would not seem disinterested, so she kept quiet. But she could not sit there any longer. When the train pulled in to Cupar station she excused herself, citing the need for air, and went to stand out in the corridor. A blast of cold wind came from an open exterior door, bringing with it the smell of rain. Now that the train was standing still at the platform, the full force of the gale outside could be both heard and felt. The whole carriage rocked and reeled.

"Welcome to Scotland, miss," the soft voice said

from her left. Once again he stood with the light at his back such that his face was hidden in shadow. "How are you enjoying it so far?"

She felt like running to him... throwing herself into his arms and be damned with the consequences. But she could almost feel Pater's gaze at her back, holding her rigid in her place, defining the flow of her life for the long stretch of future to come.

"It is not what I imagined," she said softly.

"*Love swells like the Solway, but ebbs like its tide*," the tall man whispered in return.

"Do not tease me with Scott," she said, suddenly angry. "Not when Pater has betrothed me to... to..."

"*I come in peace to dance at your bridal*," he said, his voice like soft silk.

Julia was in no mood for games.

"What is it you want of me, sir?" she said, raising her voice to be heard above the wind that suddenly raised up a notch.

"What is it you want of me?" the soft voice replied.

Her heart knew the answer, and beat ever faster. But Pater was still watching, and she could not bring herself to disobey him quite so openly.

Not yet.

A small voice had said that in her mind, but it seemed her tall companion had once more guessed her intentions.

"I will be here," he said. "I will always be here. Five and seventy, three score and fifteen, a long span come to a sudden end, as they all do, in darkness and turmoil. It's coming yet, for a' that."

She wanted to go to him, but Pater's gaze continued

to hold her.

The tall man acted for her. He moved forward, so close that she might touch him if she chose. She still could not see his face, but she felt his soft breath at her cheek as he leaned towards her and planted a kiss there, cold and dusty, but a kiss none the less.

She heard movement behind her and turned. Pater was already out of his seat and coming towards her. He pulled the carriage door open with such force that it slammed hard against the wall, the noise echoing in the corridor even above the wind.

"You must go," she said, then realized that her companion had already left. She looked up and down the corridor but there was no sign of him.

"Was that a man?" Pater hissed at her, the anger red in his face. "Was it?"

Pater dragged her back inside the carriage. As he pulled the door closed behind him the train pulled out of Cupar Station.

Over the next ten minutes Julia tried very hard to keep her attention on George, but the youth just could not stop talking about himself; about his prowess at shooting, his ability to make money, his horses, his dogs, even his taste in leather footwear. She was already weary of him.

And Pater wants me to spend years like this?

George finally realized that he did not have Julia's full attention, and the look of anger that crossed his face told her more than she needed to know about him. She resolved that she would have it out with Pater as soon as they were alone. She could *never* marry this boy.

Not when there is a man in the corridor waiting for

me.

The thought came unbidden, but she found it to be most agreeable, and lost herself in a reverie of thoughts of soft voices and even softer kisses. She was brought back to harsh reality when Pater poked her in the ribs.

"What is the matter with you tonight, girl? Young George here has asked you a question. Please at least have the good manners to answer him."

She blushed.

"I am sorry, Pater," she said, the lie coming easily to her lips. "I was just excited at the thought of the bridge."

Across the carriage from her, George's scowl turned quickly to a broad smile. He stood and reached for her hand.

"Then come. We are almost there. We shall watch from the window."

His hand felt like a cold sausage as he took her by the wrist and led her out to the corridor. Her tall companion was nowhere to be seen and she felt her heart sink.

George in the meantime had become as excited as a puppy at walk-time.

But far less endearing.

"It is a great wonder. The cylindrical cast iron columns supporting the long span of the bridge are each seventy five yards long, and Thomas Bouch received a knighthood for the design," he said. "Imagine. A knighthood."

She could indeed imagine. She was thinking of her tall stranger again.

There never was a knight like the young Lochinvar.

George failed to notice her lack of interest and led her to a window on the far side away from the wind and rain. Here the sound of the wheels on the rails was more audible, even above the storm.

George was still lost in his own monologue.

"We should see the lights of the city across the river from here. 'Tis a pity it is so inclement. It is a fine view by moonlight."

There was a movement in the corridor behind them, little more than a slight dimming of the light, but Julia turned eagerly, anticipating her *Lochinvar*.

George tugged at her wrist, dragging her closer towards the window. "What is the matter with you, girl?"

The tone, the assumption of *ownership* so exactly mirrored that of her pater that Julia pulled herself away, almost dragging them both off balance as the train *lurched*.

The wheels screeched on the rails and metal squealed.

The tall stranger was suddenly by her side, as if from nowhere. And now she could see his eyes, pale blue and infinitely sad in a dark skinned face that spoke of long days under the sun.

"Will you come, lass? It is time. Five and seventy, three score and fifteen, a long span come to a sudden end, as they all do, in darkness and turmoil. It's coming yet, for a' that."

The carriage suddenly fell sidewards, throwing George and Julia off balance. She found herself in the arms of the stranger, suddenly warm and cosy.

"What is it that you want of me?" he whispered.

She looked at George, who was too busy clinging desperately to a wildly swaying door to pay her any attention.

"The poor craven bridegroom said never a word," the tall stranger intoned, and laughed, a sound so sweet that Julia could not help but laugh along with him.

"Yes, I will come," she said, just as the window behind them fell in with a crash of glass. She blinked, just once, then seemed to be looking down from a great height. The train was halfway across a long bridge, and already falling from the rails. Tall towers of iron buckled and bent in the wind, throwing metal and stone down to the foaming waters far below.

She remembered George's words.

The cylindrical cast iron columns supporting the long span of the bridge are each seventy five yards long.

"Five and seventy, three score and fifteen, a long span come to a sudden end, as they all do, in darkness and turmoil," her companion whispered.

She lay her head against his chest, listening to the thrum of his wings against the wind.

"Now tread we a measure," she said softly, as the Tay Bridge fell into the river far below.

A Slim Chance

He was thin, thinner than anyone I had ever seen who was still ambulatory.

"I'm Ian Duncan, and I need your help," he said as he pushed open my office door that morning – it took him three tries and the door only opened when he put a shoulder into it to help his arms.

"I can see that," I said. "Come and sit down before you blow away."

He sat in the chair opposite me, perched on the edge as if afraid it might swallow him whole. I thought about offering him a cigarette, but decided against it – the shock to his system might be too much. I sat back and let him talk.

"It was four months ago. There were six of us then, and it started as a dare. One of those *Comic Relief* shows was coming up, and we decided to go on a diet for charity. That first week we lost six pounds between us... at least, the five guys did. Wee Annie Gardner struggled though. She just couldn't take to the exercise and..."

I coughed politely.

"Is there a point to this, Mr. Duncan?"

"I need you for protection," he said quietly. "Protection against what's after me."

It was my turn to sigh.

"And just what *is* after you?" I asked. "Some big dog? Or a Glesga heavy with an axe maybe?"

The fear lay big in his eyes.

"It's worse," he said. "Much worse. Three of my

friends died recently. And I might be next," he said.

"Tell me," I said softly.

He started to cry in that *holding-it-all-in* way kids do when they're trying to be brave. His shoulders heaved and tears ran down his cheeks. Then he *really* frightened me. He started to wheeze, struggling for air. He doubled over and broke into a coughing fit so strong I thought his lungs might come up.

I poured a glass of whisky and held it out to him, having to place it in his shaking hand.

He downed it in one. The coughing stopped. But the fear was back in his eyes as he stared at the glass.

"I thought it was water," he whispered.

Something stronger than just the wind rattled my window behind me.

"Please. I thought it was water," he shouted. He got out of the chair so fast that it fell with a *bang* on the floor.

I stood, unsure as to what to do next.

I wasn't given an option. The window behind me blew in with a crash and a spatter of glass. I felt something grab me at the back of the neck, and my head was thrust down, hard, against the side of the desk. The corner caught me near the right eye. Blood spurted as I fell away.

Duncan screamed.

I tried to wipe my eyes clear. I was partly blinded by blood in one eye, and my sight was blurred, but I could make out enough to know that something large and white crouched over the man.

What the hell is that?

Duncan stopped screaming and went quiet. The only

sound was a moist *sucking* like a wet fart. I wanted to stand up straight but my head had other ideas and the room span until I steadied myself with a hand on my desk.

Now even the sucking noise had stopped.

I looked up as the out-of-focus white thing bounded off Duncan and came towards me. I just had time to duck as it leapt over the desk like a pony taking a jump. By the time I'd turned it had gone out the window. My sight cleared... enough that I was able to pick my way through the shards of glass on my way to the window. I looked out, but there was only the usual Glasgow skyline.

Duncan lay still on the floor. I staggered to his side. His eyes stared up at me from a face that had dried out like an old raisin left in the sun.

He was dead and already going cold.

I lifted the money from the desk and, closing the door quietly behind me, went to work.

~-o0O0o-~

My first stop was the Twa Dugs. I told George what I needed and he gave me an elastoplast, a beer and his promise that he'd get the mess cleared up.

"How did he find you?" I asked George as I sipped at the beer. The urge was to knock it down and get started on the next, but Duncan had laid his money down. That bought him my attention, for a while at least.

George shrugged.

"How does anybody find me? You ken what this

town is like."

I knew only too well.

Everybody knows everything when there's money involved and nothing when there's Polis in the frame.

I thanked George for the beer and headed for the Mitchell library.

I thought I'd had a headache to start with, but two hours at the microfiche taught me the real meaning of the word. But I found what I was looking for. Anne Gardner, 31, from Clarkston, was found dead in her flat on the twenty-second of February. The cause of death was listed as starvation but the Procurator Fiscal had delivered an open verdict... she'd been perfectly fit and healthy the night before, and had been seen tucking into a few beers and a curry in a restaurant off Sauchiehall Street. I found out more than I needed to know about her from the tabloid reports of her death, but I also found out where she had worked.

The office was in the old Merchant area in the town centre. Not that many years ago this had been a place of dark dank tenements with hookers on the corners and winos in the alleys. Now it stood as a shining market of consumerism with Italian clothes shops, coffee bars and chrome and glass offices for people in expensive suits.

At this time of night it was mostly shut and locked down. What the suits didn't know was that the winos and hookers hadn't gone. They'd just changed their shift patterns. Down in the alleys at night the waste from the rich became the tit-bits of the poor as scavengers raked over the detritus of the day.

Nothing really changes.

The security guard at Carnegie Towers wasn't keen

on me until I showed him the quarter bottle of whisky I kept in my coat for such occasions. That loosened his tongue, and a fifty from Duncan's pile made sure it stayed that way.

"I didnae ken the Gardner lassie," he said. "But I was there the nicht the other two got deid."

I handed him the bottle and let him talk.

"Everybody knew about the diet team," he said. "They were making fools o' themselves in the wee gym downstairs every night. Thirty and forty year old men trying to be boys again, and failing. The lass dying put a wee bit of a dampner on them for a while, but a couple of weeks later they were back at it as bad as ever.

"The night it happened two of them were down there, each trying to lift heavier weights than the other. The three of us were the only ones in the building and I was jist waiting for them to go before I could lock up and have a kip. They buggered that idea when they came straight out the shower and ordered fish suppers. They gave me a tenner to go get them and told me to keep the change, but I was still pissed off later when they called down from the office.

"They wanted me to go up and get rid of a big white cat that was pestering them. I told them to fucking catch it for themselves.

"I didna hear a peep out of them after that.

"When I did my rounds at ten o'clock I found them baith, face down in their supper. The doctors said they'd starved. But whit dae doctors know? Everybody kens ye cannae starve while eating a fish supper. It's jist no' natural."

~-ooOOoo-~

That seemed to be the sum total of his knowledge. I didn't know yet how it helped me, but my *spidey* sense was tingling.

The game was afoot.

I did get something else of interest... I got the last known addresses of the remaining three dieters. It had been a while since any of them had been seen at work, but the guard didn't seem too concerned.

"Yon Duncan man was here longer than the others. But everybody was glad when he called to say he wasn't coming back. He was getting too skinny anyway," he said as I left him with the last of the booze. "He was scary."

I already knew where Duncan had ended up. That just left the last two... Peter Clarke and David Ellison. Both had addresses out in Milngavie... too far for a trip at this time of the night. The pounding in my head had lessened, but it hadn't gone away, and the small amount of whisky I'd taken from the quarter bottle had just got me started.

I *should* have headed back to the office and the bed in the back room. But all that waited there for me was Duncan's dead eyes. They'd still be there, even if George had cleaned up the mess. I needed a drink before I'd be prepared to face it. I wandered down towards Central Station, found a bar that had avoided gentrification, and settled in.

I have little memory of the next few hours. I drank, I talked to strangers, and I drank some more. I drank until my head stopped pounding and I couldn't see Ian

Duncan's eyes.

Some time later I slept.

I dreamed of white cats and fish suppers.

~-o0O0o-~

When I woke it was morning, and I was sitting on a bench in Buchanan Street Bus Station. My mouth felt like somebody had shat in it. I took a taxi back to the office and climbed the stairs as wearily as Duncan had managed the day before.

George at the Twa Dugs had been as good as his word. There was no dead body on the floor, and the window was fixed. The room smelled of putty. I sent some cigarette smoke to join it before showering and shaving.

After two cups of coffee I started to feel almost human. The weight of Duncan's money started once again to prey on my conscience. I lit up a new Camel, pulled the phone towards me and went back to work.

Clarke and Ellison weren't hard to find in the book, but Clarke wasn't answering the phone, and I got the answering machine at Ellison's place. I wasn't doing anyone any good by sitting in the office, so I left a message for Ellison telling him I was on the way and headed for Milngavie.

It had just started to rain so I hailed a cab. He wasn't keen on going so far out of the city, but the sight of my money shut him up fast. We headed along Great Western Road past Anniesland, and the traffic lessened as we left the city behind.

This far out Glasgow becomes suburbia. Neat houses

with neat cars outside and neat little people inside, living neat, tidy lives of clockwork regularity.

For people out here, the Glasgow I knew was a foreign country. They visited it during their working hours, but they only saw what was on the surface, what the city let them see. They didn't remember that all around them was a dark, old lady, brooding and cold. She mostly let herself show at nights, in the bars, around the docklands, and in the vast cemeteries which marked where all her children lay sleeping.

Some of them might occasionally catch a glimpse of her, in the face of a drunk, in the hands of a beggar. But they'd soon forget her once safely home and locked into their havens with their soap operas and reality shows and their TV dinners and boxes of Australian wine.

I was never allowed to forget her.

And I don't want to.

The cab dropped me off in a cul-de-sac of houses that all looked the same... perfectly groomed, perfectly dull. Curtains twitched as I walked up the drive to Ellison's place. A trim woman in a nurse's uniform answered the door.

"I knew the suburbs were kinky," I said. "But isn't this taking it a bit far?"

I didn't even get a smile.

"If you're here to see Mr. Ellison, he's resting, and can't be disturbed."

"He's expecting me."

She looked me up and down.

"He's expecting a private detective, not somebody who smells like a brewery and looks like he's slept in one.

"I left a message..." I said.

She sighed loudly and rolled her eyes. She looked kind of cute, but not enough for me to cut her any slack. I stared at her until she relented.

"He got it," she finally said. "He said I was to show you in."

She stood aside, but only just, and the look she gave me told me *just* what she thought of the idea. She motioned me through to a front room that had been turned into a room to care for a *very* sick man.

Ellison lay on a bed that looked far too big for him. He reminded me of the children you see in pictures of African famines; distended belly pushing through hospital whites, arms like thin sticks, lips pale, drawn back from grey gums showing yellowed, tombstone teeth.

"He won't let me put in a drip," she said. "Won't let me feed him. All he has is water."

"How long has he got?"

She shrugged. She looked like she was past caring.

"By rights he should be dead already."

One of the stick-like arms rose and waved me forward. I had to lean over close to hear him, and even then his voice barely rose above a whisper.

"Tell Clarke I don't forgive him," he said.

"For what?"

He coughed and spluttered, thin spots of blood splattering the white of his covers.

"It was Clarke's idea in the first place," he said. "Him and that fucking binding agreement he made us sign."

The man laughed bitterly, and I realized he was

hardly more than thirty years old. He looked at least eighty.

"It was binding all right. And now there's just the two of us left. Well you can tell Clarke that I might be dying... but I'll see him go to hell first."

He started to laugh and cackle and I realized something else... the poor bugger was mad as a bag of rabid monkeys. More blood spattered. The nurse ushered me aside as the coughing fit got worse and some of the machines he was wired to started to beep faster.

At the back of the room French doors opened out into the garden. I went out and lit up a smoke.

The case was getting to me. I hadn't learned anything I liked, and little that would lead me to the root of what was going on. Meanwhile everybody involved was heading south fast.

The nurse came out five minutes later and bummed a cigarette from me.

"How's the patient?" I asked as I lit her up.

She sucked a lung-full before replying. "He coughed himself unconscious," she said. "He won't last but a few more days. Maybe a wee bit more now that I've put a drip in... he cannae complain when he's out for the count."

And just like that everything came together... Duncan drinking my whisky, Wee Annie eating a curry, the two men wolfing down fish suppers. Somebody... or something, didn't want any breaking of the diet.

Binding agreement.

That's what Ellison had said. It looked like it had been more binding than any of them had anticipated.

I turned back into the room. "You have to take the drip out," I said.

"I don't *have* to do anything."

We weren't given time to get into an argument. The front window blew in with a crash and something that looked like a shaved albino chimpanzee bounded inside. I was halfway to the bed already, but I was too late. It latched its mouth on Ellison's face and *sucked*.

The sound of Ellison's life draining away made my guts roil. I stepped forward and punched at the hunched figure sat on the man's chest. My hand seemed to sink into it. It felt like hitting a slab of warm butter.

The moist sucking stopped. The beast raised its mouth from the dry husk that had once been David Ellison. It turned towards me.

There was no face.

But it saw me, just the same.

A wet, oily mouth opened, no more than a slit in that formless visage. I aimed another punch, but met only air as the beast leapt out of the broken window. I had a last glimpse of white as it jumped through the shrubbery, then it was gone.

~-o0O0o-~

The nurse stood at the garden door, cigarette dangling from her fingers, mouth opening and closing like a drowning goldfish.

"I thought he was hallucinating," she whispered. "A big white dug he said it was. I didnae believe him."

I took the cigarette from her before she burned her fingers.

"His pal, Peter Clarke. Does he live round here?"

She couldn't take her eyes from the dried out *thing* on the bed.

'I thought he was addled," she said softly. She was on the verge of going into shock, but I didn't have time to play nice. I slapped her cheek until I got her attention. It took a while.

Finally her eyes fixed on mine.

"Clarke," I said. "Does he live round here?"

"Acacia Avenue," she said. "Two lefts then a right, number 45."

I was on my way out of the door before she remembered to be outraged.

"Hey. You hit me. I've a good mind to..."

I didn't hear any more. I ran along the suburban streets, hoping like hell I would make it on time.

~-o0O0o-~

45 Acacia Avenue wasn't quite like the other houses on the street. The lawn hadn't been mown for months, and fast food cartons lay strewn the length of the drive alongside torn rubbish bags spilling their contents to the wind.

But it was the front door that gave away the fact that I'd left suburbia behind. It was covered in intricate drawings done in black charcoal; swirls and curlicues around pentagrams and hexagrams. I'd seen something like it before, during research on another case that had taken a dive into the twilight zone. But this looked less like a formal magic protection ritual and more like a man trying as many symbols as he could, in the hope that at least one might work.

I knocked hard on the door.

Somebody moved inside, but they didn't answer.

"Mr. Clarke? I know about the diet... and the *Binding Agreement.* I'm here to help."

"Help? I'm afraid the time for that passed a while back."

The door opened.

I expected to see another skeletal, shuffling figure, but this man was portly, almost fat. He was unshaven and smelled ripe, but otherwise seemed healthy.

"Peter Clarke?"

He hurried me inside and closed the door quickly. He led me through to a room piled knee deep in food cartons, beer cans and dirty clothing. It smelled worse than I did after a night on the town. The curtains had been pulled closed and the air felt stale and warm. There hadn't been a window opened in here for a long time.

"It's the maid's day off," he said, and spilled a waterfall of trash on the floor to make room for me to sit on an armchair. I let myself down gingerly, making sure I was going to be able to get back up before committing myself.

I lit up a smoke as soon as he sat opposite me. It helped some with the smell, but not quite enough.

We sat and looked at each other for a while.

"You're looking well," I said when he showed no signs of talking.

"In the circumstances, I suppose I can't really complain. I could be dead, like the other three."

"Other five," I said softly.

He went pale.

"I'm the last?"

I nodded.

"Then it must be *huge* by now," he said.

I didn't have to ask him what he meant.

"I've seen it," I said. "But I don't know exactly what I was looking at. Care to fill me in?"

He lifted a six pack of beer and threw a can towards me. I was careful to give it a good wipe with the arm of my jacket before opening it. It was warm, but went down well enough.

"It was Duncan's fault," he began. "We were just a few days into the diet and we started talking about targets. Between the six of us we decided to lose around ten stone.

"'That's a full person's worth,' Duncan had said. And that's what got me thinking that we should make ourselves a promise. So I had the contract written up, that we would go on until enough weight was lost to add up to a person. It was my idea that we sign it in blood, to seal the deal."

He laughed bitterly.

"It was supposed to be a joke... just something to focus our attention. How was I to know that it wasn't all bullshit?"

"Well, you know now," I replied. I lit a second cigarette.

"I had an inkling when Annie died," he said. "And then when the other two were taken at the office, I knew something was up. So I did some reading. Two nights later something scratched at my door after I'd had my supper, but I'd taken precautions and put up the protection. And it's kept working."

"You've been here ever since?"

He waved at the detritus around us. "Welcome to my world."

"And you knew how to stop this thing, but you let it take your friends anyway?"

He shrugged.

"I figured if it was pestering them, then it wasn't pestering me. Besides, if they had any smarts of their own, they could have figured it out the same way I did."

I was getting angry now, and had to push it down. "They died horrible, piteous deaths you wouldn't wish on your worst enemy."

He shrugged again.

"Shit happens," he said.

I had nothing more to say to this *thing*. The white beast had more humanity in it than he would ever have.

I stood and walked to the front door. He followed me and stood in the hallway.

"So you have no regrets for their deaths?"

"Survival of the fittest," he said. "I win."

He closed the door on me.

I turned to leave.

It stood there in the shadows beside the small porch... a white figure as tall as a man but unformed, featureless save for a gaping maw of a mouth. It swayed from side to side and keened in a high wailing like a child's sob.

Survival of the fittest.

I turned back to the front door and wiped a smudge down the length of the protection spell. Then I walked away. I heard the door crash inwards as I reached the end of the driveway.

I might only have imagined that I heard the screams.

But I smiled anyway.

William Meikle is a Scottish writer, now living in Canada, with twenty novels published in the genre press and over 300 short story credits in thirteen countries. His work has appeared in a number of professional anthologies and magazines. He lives in Newfoundland with whales, bald eagles and icebergs for company. When he's not writing he dreams of fortune and glory.

Connect with William Meikle

Website:
www.williammeikle.com
Facebook:
www.facebook.com/williammeikle
Twitter:
twitter.com/williemeikle
Amazon:
www.amazon.com/author/williammeikle

Connect with Crystal Lake Publishing

Website (be sure to sign up for our newsletter):
www.crystallakepub.com
Facebook:
www.facebook.com/Crystallakepublishing
Twitter:
https://twitter.com/crystallakepub

We hope you enjoyed this title. If so, we would be grateful if you could leave a review on Amazon, Goodreads, your blog or one of the many websites open to book reviews. Reviews are essential for a successful book. And remember to keep an eye out for more of our books. We have collections by Daniel I. Russell, Kevin Lucia and Gary McMahon, a novella by Paul Kane and a couple of anthologies.

THANK YOU FOR PURCHASING THIS BOOK

www.ingramcontent.com/pod-product-compliance
Lightning Source LLC
Chambersburg PA
CBHW070905180626
46817CB00003B/930